THE
SQUARE

Ed Adams

a firstelement production

First published in Great Britain in 2020 by firstelement
Copyright © 2020 Ed Adams
Directed by thesixtwenty

10 9 8 7 6 5 4 3 2 1

A CIP catalogue record for this book is available from the
British Library.
All rights reserved.

ISBN: 978-1-9163383-8-8
ISBN-eBook : 978-1-9163383-9-5

Printed and bound in Great Britain by Ingram Spark

Ed Adams
an imprint of firstelement.co.uk
ed.adams@Ed-Adams.net
rashbre@mac.com

Mailing list: https://mailchi.mp/9f0b30712620/ed_adam

THANKS

A big thank you for the tolerance and bemused support from all of those around me, especially Julie who has to make up the excuses. To the readers of my prior novels and to the requests for further frolics from Bigsy, Clare and Jake.

This novel bridges the dots from The Triangle to The Circle, although the circumstances of its writing are more in keeping with Pulse.

When I started this, I didn't expect to be in lockdown with crashed money markets and a mystery virus on the loose. Stranger things can happen in fiction, I suppose.

And, of course, thanks to the extensive support via the scribbles of rashbre via http://rashbre2.blogspot.com and its cast of amazing and varied readers whether human, twittery, smoky, cool kats, photographic, dramatic, musical, anagrammed, globalized or simply maxed-out.

Time to put on a tune and enjoy the ride with the cast of characters involved in producing this, whether real or imaginary

And Thanks, of course, to you, dear reader, for at least 'giving it a go'.

To Christina Nott

PART ONE

Ed Adams

Sand

"in every grain of sand there is the story of the earth"

— Rachel Carson

Cairo

16:00 Eastern European Time (EET).

James expected this to be a short, sharp mission. He'd be paid and out of here in another couple of hours. He'd hand over the bag and be gone.

He sheltered on the edge of a dune. The vestigial grass had a razor-sharp edge, scratching his arm as he slithered into a comfortable position. The Subaru was parked about 200 metres further away, concealed behind another dune. A long way ahead, he could see the tiny outline of the truck, heading towards him in a shimmer from the heat. It seemed to be running above the ground because of the haze and he could understand how people thought they could see water in the desert.

The truck's progress was also almost silent, and then he heard a whine from what sounded like an American military diesel engine. He'd heard the sound before, in

Germany, where there were many of these trucks used around the bases, but here it seemed displaced.

Through the sound he noticed a further noise, a slow throb which was getting louder. He looked around and could see a speck in the sky, not a bird. It was bigger and tracking the path of the truck. A helicopter, it looked like an Apache as it became closer. An attack helicopter, carrying a fair array of armaments. By now the truck was less than 800 metres away, still proceeding at a steady speed.

The Apache was low in the air, but then suddenly, but languorously, the helicopter let go of a missile. It didn't fly straight, but took a lazy path from the helicopter, like the casual throw of a soft toy from an adult to a small child.

But whatever it was, it would hit the truck. A second or so later, there was a flash, and it was as if time had moved from lazy to accelerated in a split second. As the missile hit the truck, a white flash exploded in a vertical line from the ground to two or three hundred metres in the air. The power of the explosion seemed out of proportion to the previous few seconds of activity, and James sheltered his face with his arm, the same one that had been cut a few moments earlier by the grass blade.

Now, he could hear a shrill electronic sound and he realised that the helicopter was locking on to his Subaru and was planning to vaporise it in the same way as the truck. He buried himself in the sand rather than attempting to run. That way, if the chopper was looking for vehicles, it may not spot a lone person hidden by the scratchy dune grass.

In the far distance he saw a momentary flash from the ground and a black line crossing the sky. Someone had launched a surface-to-air missile. The black trail slid through the air towards the helicopter. He heard the Apache's engine squeal as it banked first left and then right in an attempt at evasion. It was ejecting what looked like hot metal strips. But it was too late. It was still too low.

The SAM made contact with the helicopter and in a much yellower fireball than the truck's explosion he watched the helicopter drop to the desert floor. He lay low for longer in case there were any more surprises, but no, a few minutes later he was preparing his escape in the Subaru, alert to the thought that whoever fired the surface-to-air may head his way.

As he climbed into the car, he scratched his arm, remembering the grass, but as he looked down, he noticed that his arm was bright red as if scalded and that the hairs on his arm looked as if they had been shaved. At least one blast had been close enough to have scorched him. He felt his hair and noticed that part was matted, also from the blast. It had been a close thing. He floored the pedal, skittering back onto the road, heading away from the direction of the surface missile.

The Square

Two hundred kilometres away, in Cairo, Karen Martin was sitting in the Hilton, sipping a drink in the Belvedere. She was waiting for a call from James to confirm that the exchange had taken place. It was supposed to happen at four thirty in the afternoon, and now it was nearly five o'clock. This was not a pleasurable part of the plan. She had wanted to accompany James to the drop, but he had urged caution in case of unexpected events. Karen had access to further resources and by doing it this way there was no obvious trail to follow to link them together. Then suddenly, her cell phone started to warble.

She flipped the phone open.

"Yes?" she enquired.

"James" came the reply.

"We have a problem. I'm on my way back. Without the invoice," continued James.

Karen knew this meant something was wrong, but that James was not in immediate danger.

"Usual place," said Karen.

The place they had arranged to meet was far from 'their usual place' but was a safe and random place within the town. They had chosen it whilst James sat in a bar and pointed to a map of Cairo. Their plan was to use the meeting point on a signalled date at a predetermined time. That time was 6.30 in the evening, when there would be a good number of people around to mask their meeting. So, the meeting would be tomorrow.

Karen would move from the Hilton in the next few minutes. She had booked into two different hotels as a general precaution when she first arrived and would now move to the other hotel while remaining checked in at the first one. This was to help hide the trail. The activity would be good and take her mind off the next three hours whilst James made his way back to Cairo. She knew that his route would be slow because of the desert, but that once James was back on the main roads, he should speed up.

She would not know what had happened until the next day, but at the moment needed to keep a low profile and not attract attention. Another fifteen minutes and she was leaving the hotel, not taking bags and careful to leave her existing hotel room looking occupied. She needed to be in the new hotel, but without the discovery that she had moved.

Karen was using basic tradecraft. She knew that with an operation like the current one it was less menacing when she was the contact and ostensibly alone for the meeting with James.

She needed to know the location of the car and cases which James would provide and then hand the operation along to others to complete the exchange. Clean and clinical. She was the only one to directly meet James;

The Square

James wouldn't see the rest of the team and they wouldn't see him. No direct contact and no physical contact with the goods. A cellular handover.

Karen suspected that this was a bigger situation than the exchange of the cases. Her boss, Robert Alton, had called her in for a briefing about this a few days ago, but had kept the entire mission very compartmentalised. She would know the transit team behind her, but for this one she just had another phone number.

Karen knew that the major aspects of her missions seemed to relate to the fronting role she had in this current situation. Sitting about in hotels, finding contacts and marshalling resources.

Occasionally she had to meet a target to relay a message. Nothing messy, dangerous, or difficult. And through doing this she had visited Washington, Helsinki, Toronto, Switzerland, Paris and Munich.

Unlike what she had expected, she often used her own name and passport, and appeared to have a travelling sales role for a marketing company. It was all very plausible and low key.

This was the first mission where the false identity was an absolute pre-requisite. Richard Alton had been insistent.

Karen made her phone call to the support team. "We haven't got the invoice." She hung up and removed the battery and sim card from the phone.

-.-- . ... --..-- / .. - / .. ... / -- --- .-. ... . / -.-. --- -.. .

James continued the drive. The Subaru had a four-wheel drive and dealt effortlessly with the trail leading back to normal roads. He kept within speed limits and made his way towards Cairo. His concern was that the car may have been recognised by the helicopter, but they would have needed to radio in some details before the missile had destroyed them. He considered it unlikely and that he had a very high chance to be undetected. He cast an eye over his shoulder to the machined case he had been given to exchange for the ones in the truck.

He'd known it was a special mission when he had noticed the USB operated electronic lock on the case.

As he arrived back in Cairo, he headed for the quieter back area of his hotel's parking lot. James checked the car again for transmitters using a small gadget which could detect GPS, Wi-fi, Tetra and simple beaconing and everything seemed to be passive. He had done this when he left for the mission but needed to check again because of the unexpected events in the desert.

James glanced at the space blanket in the trunk. It contained a metallised core and would have been used to envelop the two small cases he had expected to receive.

Back in his room, he swept the security detector across his own clothes. He showered and swapped to another complete set of clothes before taking his original clothes to a hotel rubbish skip. Anything to minimise detection.

James hated the delay in this assignment. Whatever he should have collected was important and wanted by others but was now also vaporised from the helicopter missile.

James resigned himself to the thought he may not get paid for this work. It suited him to be freelance, to switch the work on and off, but the payments were results driven and no bags would mean no fee. However, James knew that Karen worked for the UK Government. It boosted his chances of payment considerably. Not all the money, but two thirds. The Americans were not so helpful. They might not even come to a follow-up meeting in similar circumstances.

James had already opted out of any second stage to this mission. It would be easy enough for the people organising things to get a replacement for him, and now that there was a risk, they had spotted him, it was not sensible to continue. James was a professional and knew, unlike in the movies, that if you fail a drop or a mission, it is many times safer to walk away and let an unfamiliar person take over as a replacement.

James had his brief speech ready for this, but also knew that his controller Karen would expect this.

He checked his watch. He had a set time to meet Karen and wanted to be prepared. He would take his pistol and knife, but travel light, so that if he needed to move away from the area quickly, then he would be able to.

He positioned his car in an area close to the rendezvous point. The Subaru was noticeable now, on account of the dust and desert on the paintwork, which on such a new-looking vehicle looked somewhat out of keeping. He drove the car through the complicated streets of Cairo and found a good place to park close to the embassy district. He flipped out a French CD paper for the front windshield, which made the vehicle look suitably authorised, although by doing this he knew he also risked being on surveillance cameras.

Then James walked out into the streets of Cairo. The nearby offices in their skyscrapers gave it the looks of a modern and rapidly expanding city, but James knew that much of the centre was ancient and labyrinthine.

Without the air conditioning of the car, he noticed the thick air immediately. The effects of what was happening around choked the central area. Beset with environmental problems, there were old and highly polluting cars and taxis creating a permanent yellow and orange smog and a taste mixing dust with sand and copper.

But the main thoughts on James' mind were to get to the rendezvous. The original plan would have him hand over a small package to Karen, which was actually a decoy. He just needed to tell her the car location and registration and her accomplices would have picked it up. He would have been wired the money to a pre-designated account. Now, instead, he was using the car as part of a contingency escape plan.

At just after 6pm, he walked past the rendezvous, half an hour ahead of the meeting time. No sign of Karen, but he wondered if she was doing the same.

James scoped a couple of other roads and an alley which led down to the water's edge of the Nile. He took the alley to check its potential as another route. Sure enough, a path ran along the edge, busy with traders and tourists.

James re-checked his watch and then made his way back towards the cafe, this time expecting to see Karen in position. As he approached, he could see her sitting in the cafe's small terrace. She spotted him and started to stand.

James heard a crack and saw her move sharply to the left, as if she had been punched very hard. Then another crack and he saw her lifted into the air about two feet off the ground and propelled into the next table, causing cups and plates to fall to the ground.

He looked to his right and realised Karen's assailant was using a high velocity rifle from a nearby rooftop. He looked back towards her and saw that she was now on the ground, but that everyone around her had scattered.

James thought quickly. Karen identified him, but he had not signalled back, and at the time she stood up a professional marksman had shot her.

James knew it was better to move away, out of the kill-zone, but without drawing attention to himself. Instead of turning, he crossed the road diagonally as if in the same direction but was now under the awning of some nearby shops. The one on the corner was a food store. He walked in, feeling a blast of air-conditioned air and a carbon taste of air filters.

He walked directly to the back of the store and through two rubberised semi-transparent spring doors into what was the loading area at the back of the shop. He kept going through a concreted back yard and onto a busy street.

Several taxis parked in a row. He climbed into the first one and asked for the airport. It was an old car, no air-conditioning and wind-down windows in the back. He felt the heat from the seats and opened the windows to force in more air. Cairo blurred past. James was only thinking back to the scene at the cafe, of Karen, and whether he was now in danger.

James knew he needed to make himself invisible. He couldn't risk going back to the U.K. or even back to Paris. So much for this being a routine pickup and exchange. He should have known that there could be trouble when he was quoted the high fee for the work. He knew that he provided extra trustworthy insulation between the goods and their eventual recipient, but not that there would be determined forces in pursuit.

He quickly analysed the situation. The UK Government had requested a pickup but needed it to be anonymous. The main operation was in Egypt, so it was likely to be something with a middle eastern origin. Just pass the package to the Brits.

Except. They had intercepted the truck carrying the package. By whom? But then the helicopter had been destroyed. Another group? And then his U.K. contact had been shot in the rendezvous cafe.

He thought he had escaped detection through all of this. His best plan was now to be as far from Cairo as quickly as possible.

He fiddled with the strap on the small day sack he was carrying. Just credit cards, identities, passports, cash and a few other essentials. He could retrieve a couple of other items from the parked car. There was too much risk in returning to the hotel.

He had been careful with the car and hotel room. They were both on credit cards and there would be an automatic charge through to the end of the week. He would phone the car rental company from the airport to state its location. He would say it had broken down, and he had caught a taxi. The car firm would send someone to move the car – they would be pleased to be able to start it and its removal would reduce his probability of detection.

He decided that the United States was a good option and would allow him time to re-gain his thoughts and work out the next part of his plan. If he could get to New York, he had a superb place to stay, off of the radar.

He reminded himself of the need to stay focussed. His chief objective was to get out, and to get his identity adapted. As he turned towards the airline terminals, two local 'helpers' walked forward to assist him with his backpack, to make a few euros. A small guy to lift his bag and a big guy to enforce collection of a 'service charge'.

They backed away when they saw his eyes, "Don't even think about it."

 Soon James was through the mayhem of the airport and on the plane, sitting back in a business class seat. As he eased back in the seat, he could feel the tiredness sweep over him. It was like someone was draining all the energy out at a speed he could almost feel rush through his body. He knew this was just a reaction to the events of the last few days. His brain was telling his body that it was now okay to relax, and the ten hours to fly to New York would give him a chance to plan his next moves.

In the short term, New York provided a suitable haystack for him to hide within, whilst he figured out what was happening. The plane taxied, accelerated, rotated and was airborne. James was already asleep.

London

"Being a seasoned Londoner, he gave the body the "London once-over"

- a quick glance to determine whether this was a drunk, a crazy or a human being in distress.

The fact that it was entirely possible for someone to be all three simultaneously is why good-Samaritanism in London is considered an extreme sport –

like BASE jumping or crocodile wrestling."

— Ben Aaronovitch (Midnight Riot)

SI6

Robert Alton had been reading routine information feeds from his office in SI6.

He'd just seen an unverified incident from Cairo. Some sort of shooting. He knew that SI6 had an operation in that area.

SI6 was the special operations unit dedicated to homeland security of the United Kingdom. Many people had heard of MI5, although Alton thought the real action was with SI6, who were involved in special operations when things were likely getting out of hand.

On average, there were between twenty and thirty special operations running related to terrorist related situations. A dozen years ago, it had been around ten operations and half of those involved Ireland.

Nowadays there was a full spectrum of countries involved, with Middle East, Afghanistan and Africa high on the list. Ireland still featured but was a small percentage of where the time was spent.

Robert Alton had been with the unit for about five years and after the bewildering rush of situations when he joined, he was now good at identifying the serious situations.

He was also directly involved with complex events. Since the emergence of internet and satellite television and the increased use of digital mobile phones, most aspects of security and surveillance had actually become more straightforward. There was a lot more computer power involved, but the systems could sense and decode many more topics.

The Americans had started a couple of big data analysis projects, got legal backing, and now the U.K. could follow in their footsteps. It was high tech, although the ability to sift to find things was still often 'after the fact', unless the agencies received a direct tip-off.

A recent intelligence coming in from the security people at GCHQ Cheltenham, England was about a series of plots related to destabilising central London. There was no clear basis for the attack, but the underlying reason seemed to relate to a fanatical unit protesting about the demise of the state of Mesopotamia. It all sounded esoteric and the work of 'crazies', but there still needed to be an investigation.

Robert was to work with Karen Martin on this assignment. Karen was her field name, and they had worked together several times.

Robert Alton clicked a speakerphone, "Can someone update me on the Cairo situation? There's been a shooting?"

"We have more information, via the local police. A lone woman, sitting in a cafe, shot twice by sniper's bullets. High velocity. Fatal. The local police are on the scene. It was close to the French Embassy. Nationality unknown."

Alton flipped the phone off. He knew. He wouldn't be close to what Karen had been doing, but he was sure that it was her mission that had been terminated. His own knowledge gap would mean there was deniability. The shooting would be written up as a senseless act of violence.

He pulled up the file for Karen's mission onto his computer screen. He knew that Karen would keep things hidden.

The background showed a series of transmissions intercepted from Turkey. The Turks were still using a cryptography which GCHQ could already unscramble. Crypto sold to them by the Americans, who would have also intercepted the same messages.

The Square

The supposition was that a cell of Al Aktar had assembled in mainland Europe and were considering a key urban target. Two cities had been selected, Frankfurt and London, based on their financial significance.

There was no clarity about individuals involved, or the basis of the attack. The immediate thoughts had been related to aircraft-based attacks similar to the 9/11, but there was no actual intelligence to support this.

After a couple of days delay, the Turkish authorities had alerted the US and the UN and the information had rippled through to various security organisations.

Robert Alton had seen this situation before, where the security channels become so choked with the information that anyone with even vague access would know that they had discovered it. This would be a deterrent to whoever was planning the attack. The knowledge that half the world's security services were on specific alert.

So, at a first level, the subtext said this was not a real situation. That was when he had discussed a plan with Karen.

He remembered Karen's scepticism similar to his own initial analysis. Except Alton knew that the source prior to the Turkish intercept had been very strong. It came from a place that didn't break cover. It would mean that the particular network would need to cease business after sending this alert. A high price unless this was something solid.

Alton could also see that the source implicated other nation states and suggested that the funding for the attack was bigger than a typical terrorist cell.

Robert Alton had requested Karen to chase it down. Quietly, and undercover. Let the big position play out 'upstairs' which would result in the threat being written as a false alarm.

Karen had asked for support. Investigators to check the source and an 'unknown' to act as an insulation layer.

Karen's investigators had discovered that there was something in transit. Referred to as the packages. 60 small items to be shipped via Egypt, under cover of a goods load.

Alton would need to call in the investigators to find out more about their discovery. Karen's file didn't have detail of what was in the packages.

Alton knew that the rest of Karen's support team would have gone into hiding after the shooting. He would need to coax them back into the open. And get them away from Egypt.

He pressed the phone again.

The Square

"Doug, it's Richard. We have a problem; I will need some help. And someone TL4 Arab speaking. I'm thinking Muhammad? Can we meet? This will be ears only."

"Lambeth Walk?" suggested Doug, "Give me ten minutes to find Muhammad Mubarain and we'll be along, 11:30, by the snack bar."

Gerald

Most people who saw Gerald for the first time would avert their eyes.

He lived in a squat near the Balls Pond Road area of London. Gerald wryly called the area part of the up-and-coming Hoxton, but he lived by deserted warehouses and a Saturday ad-hoc marketplace where middle Europeans would attempt to sell dubious goods from cardboard cartons.

Gerald lived by his wits and scrounged a living from small errands and some petty crime.

Gerald walked around in a grey raincoat, with a knotted scarf and a trilby hat. In a clean and well-fitted version this could have made Gerald look respectable, but with the uncared-for styling that Gerald displayed, the overall impression was that of a scruffy down-and-out.

The Square

A grey, drizzling rain had persisted all day. It flattened the landscape and blurred detail. Car lights smeared and sound deadened. This was not a good rain, just a persistent one.

Gerald was shuffling back to where he lived. He looked as grey as the surroundings and blended into the general misery.

Things had not always been this way, and Gerald had gone through a good education until the point where drugs had seen him expelled from multiple schools.

The last time he just ran away and travelled south to London as a missing person. He didn't have any serious money and nowhere to live and no plans. He had been picked up at the station by a do-gooder who had helped him into a temporary hostel. There he had made contacts and become better versed in the art of street life, which was now his main means of survival.

He'd met Lucy near to the hostel, and they'd turned tricks around the back of the north London train stations to buy drug money. One cold night, for the second time, Luce had OD'd and been taken away in the ambulance. They had taken Gerald too. He later had to identify her after she had passed away. The hospital staff had a care worker present who had offered Gerald rehab.

Gerald decided he owed it to Luce to get straight and went away to a turnaround place for several weeks to break the habit.

It had worked, and they initially moved Gerald to a small hostel to get started on his climb back to civilisation.

It wasn't an easy climb, and he'd been robbed on the first night and then blamed for another robbery, which he didn't commit.

He'd decided it was better to get out and so with little clothing but with a stash of items in a Tescos supermarket trolley he had struck out to find a squat. Gerald now lived in an unheated and semi-derelict house due for demolition with several others of similar circumstance. He was now stable, if not happy, in his lot and with his life.

There was a delicate balance amongst the squatters. Most lived off the land, begging, dealing and some petty crime. There were a couple with dogs, and the rest kept their individual areas in the house. They looked after one another to keep a balance.

That was until two new people moved in. There was something incongruous about their demeanour. By rights, as squatters, they would be poor and have only their feet to walk around. These two guys had their own van, which had a recent number plate.

The Square

Gerald knew that most people like him would not have transport -or if they did it would have not be as clearly modern as this van.

Gerald monitored his recent neighbours. They seemed more purposeful than most of the people in the area. Anyone in the squat would hide their belongings or be sleeping or chilling out from cider or drug-related abuse.

Gerald knew these guys were different, and the level of their apparent industriousness combined with their relative wealth meant they were probably involved in some higher form of mischief.

They appeared to be well fed, seemed to have supplies of snack-food whenever he had seen them and seemed to be able use normal pubs whenever they wanted. Gerald thought of them as 'the geezers'.

It seemed strange that they would use the squat at all. They had a van and took it when they left to go away, often for several days at a time. Gerald could tell when they were around because the van was pretty much their only mode of transport, unless they walked to the nearby pub.

The van was parked outside on the road, but twice it had been backed gingerly across the rubble at the front of the premises right up to the main doors. The back doors of the van had been opened and something thrown inside. The first time it happened, Gerald was further away and unable to see what was happening, but this time Gerald was close enough, shielded by a low wall.

The geezers were collecting something else, unaware of Gerald's presence.

Gerald took a look in the van. Not to steal - it was too close to his doorstep, just to know more about the two guys. Maybe it was cigarettes, booze or maybe even drugs?

He climbed over the low wall and edged to the back of the van; whose doors were still open. He felt the adrenalin as he peered around the rear doors and spotted two aluminium briefcases in the whole rear compartment.

Next, he slipped onto the back flooring of the van. He reached towards the nearest case and flicked the lock. To his surprise, the little silver clasp pinged upward. Then he tried the second clasp. The same thing happened. He could open the case.

Gerald looked around and listened. He could hear his breathing sounded loud in the back of the van. Gerald was used to the area around the squat and the noises of people moving.

He could tell if anyone was close by. No sounds. He stood a little further back from the case - now at arm's length and then, carefully, he raised its lid.

The Square

Envelopes - the case contained envelopes. Not slim white ones, but thick orange-brown padded bags. He estimated there were about ten in the case. So he slipped one into his raincoat, hurriedly closed the case and made his way back to his own side of the wall.

He could hear his blood pumping in his head as he squatted down. He had taken a risk with these two guys. They were better fed and fitter than him. If they wanted to hurt him, it would be easy for them.

Gerald decided he would go further away before he opened the envelope. He did not want to be caught red-handed. Instead, he would go to another spot, just along the road. Not good as the squat, but a great hide-away. He crept out of his part of the squat and started walking along the road. He knew he was a well-known sighting in the area, so if he behaved then no-one would think anything of it.

Ten minutes later he was in his other hideaway. He pulled the envelope from his pocket. It was about the size of a half sheet of office paper. He fingered the top where it was sealed. There was nothing special about the way it had been closed.

He opened it in a way that would allow him to re-seal it if needed. This took a couple of minutes, and at the end he could pull the flap open with no tears or creases in the envelope.

He peered inside. There was a small metal container inside. It looked like it was made of machined steel, and had a rather unusual clasp at the top, which looked as if it needed a special machine to open it. He felt the weight in his hand. For its size, it was heavy, and he assumed the metal was thick. There was a small glass bulge at the top, like an indicator light, although it was not switched on. He wondered what would happen if he pressed it like a button but thought better of it.

He noticed some small writing. A serial number and the inscription "вольфрам" on the bottom of the container. He decided it was Russian but was too difficult to decipher.

Then, on the side of the container, he noticed another small inscription. It was a symbol and a number 4. He recognised the symbol from back when he played school-time computer games. It was just like the logo for a game called Bioshock.

Gerald lost his nerve to delve any further with the container. It looked expensive, well-machined and indestructible. He wondered if the glass button was a control. Would it unlock the container, or worse, would it arm it?

Whatever it was, it looked as if they designed it to protect something expensive and to avert prying eyes.

The Square

The apparent warning logo made him think it contained something dangerous. Aside from the word and the symbol, there were no other markings on the cylinder. There was nothing else in the padded envelope. He decided the container was full of something, but it was not like any drugs he had ever seen. The guys who had been handling it were planning to deliver it and the rest of the contents to a buyer somewhere.

He would hide it somewhere safe for now and await developments. No-one had seen him at the squat while the van was there, and now he had successfully moved the envelope away.

He found a special corner and wedged the envelope and its contents behind, then replacing a couple of broken boards so that the area looked undisturbed. He thought the location was especially useful because it was so totally random.

Gerald decided to take a long walk before returning to the squat. It would put distance and an apparent alibi between him and the people with the van.

Back at the squat, the loading of the van was complete. In total, six cases, no bigger than briefcases had been placed in the van. The driver was getting ready to close the doors when he noticed another member of the squat returning.

The newcomer swayed towards them, apparently looking for some cider money from the driver or his passenger. He noticed the open doors, and the pile of aluminium cases in the back and staggered towards them. The driver and his passenger looked briefly at one another and then at the man. With a sudden movement, the passenger swung his arm towards the drunk and chopped him across the neck, crumpling him to the ground.

"Let's go," said the passenger and he and the driver ambled to the cab of the van and pulled away. The drunk lay where he had fallen, in the mud of the yard behind the van.

An hour later, when Gerald returned, the drunk was still laying there, in the same position. Gerald noticed the body, and walked cautiously forward, listening for any other sounds. He could see the van tracks and boot marks where the driver and passenger had been standing and knew what had happened.

Gerald recognised fallen person as Ben and shook his shoulder. It wasn't that unusual to see Ben slumped somewhere. He had something of an alcohol problem. Gerald and Ben shared the adjacent property but usually gave each other a lot of space. Ben was breathing and slightly choking, as well as reeking of cider and something that smelled like garden compost.

Gerald gave Ben a couple more shakes until he started to groan. Whether it was alcohol or violence related was hard to tell, although it was clear that Ben was in a bad way.

The Square

"Ben?" shouted Gerald as he shook Ben's shoulder. Ben opened his eyes and spluttered, "They hit me!"

"Yeah" said Gerald, still not completely convinced, "Who?"

"I just got back," explained Ben, "I'd been drinking and when I got back here there were those two guys with their van. I was just asking them if they had some spare change for me when they hit me!"

"Are you sure that's all?" persisted Gerald.

"Oh Yeah," continued Ben, "Their van had a lot of silver cases in the back. It looked like something expensive - maybe jewellery?"

Muhammad

Muhammad Mubarain was contacted by his team boss Doug. He was being asked to meet Robert Alton off-site, although close to the main SI6 headquarters building. This was unusual, even for Robert.

Muhammad had become part of SI6 via Robert Alton, who he had first met several years ago, when they shared a train ride across Turkey. Alton had helped Muhammad and got Muhammed's papers straightened and provided initial work, largely because of Muhammad's good English mixed with knowledge of local Arabic dialects in an area of strategic military interest.

Muhammad knew his entry into SI6 was improbable, and that was quite an asset in some of the situations over the last few years.

Muhammad's family were all from Iraq but killed as part of Saddam Hussein's purges during the 1980s.

The Square

It had started when a green army truck arrived in young Mohammad's village with five or six men in the back of it.

The men walked around and used their radio to call their base. Muhammad's father had taken Muhammad to one side.

"Go now from the village," his father had said, "Don't come back. Go on your bicycle, and leave the village along the low road, the road which runs downhill. Take this bag and take this money. It is your ticket to another life. Son, however difficult this is, you must never come back here. Do you understand?"

Muhammad was a tough youth, very fit from running and climbing in the area around the village. He had strong desert craft and knew how to stay out of trouble in the scorching sun and how to find water in the cooler evenings. He knew how to drive a car, but he would not admit this to his father, because it would cause a serious amount of disciplining.

"Something bad will happen?" he asked his father, knowing the stories from other parts of his region. "Yes, son, something terrible will happen. I don't want you to be here when the rest of the troops arrive".

Muhammad nodded. He would do as his father requested, although he hated the thought, he would be alone without his family and friends. He picked up his bicycle and made his way to the edge of the village, so that the noisy troops would not notice. Then he slithered down a bank onto the low and overgrown road leading from the village, down a long sloping hill which ran for several kilometres.

On his bicycle, the gradient gave him distance without much effort and within an hour he was many kilometres from the village, now the other side of some mountain ridges. He stopped to look back. The air was silent. The heat was intense. He could see some wisps of black cloud from behind the ridges. The black clouds were coming from about where his village was located. He blinked back a tear, turned and cycled on.

Muhammad spent three weeks alone in the open. He had to break some of his religious laws along the way, neglecting prayer and stealing food to eat as he headed eventually to the north of the country and across the border into Syria, where he could pick up a freight railway line which headed into Turkey.

He had stayed on a long and very slow freight train through Nusaybin and Senyurt and then on a long slow journey across Cappadocia to Narli, which was the nearest thing he had seen to civilisation in weeks.

Narli was also a modest vacation destination, with a famous lake and some resort hotels. Muhammad had money and identity documents from the package that his father had given him, but he knew he would need to use them with great care.

In Narli, he found a hotel laundry and instead of buying clothes, he borrowed a few from the laundry bags, converting himself into a western-looking youth.

Muhammad had been awestruck with the gargantuan landscapes of the area, the enormity of the skies and the sheer awe-inspiring natural beauty of the area sculpted by volcanoes.

Like those before him, Muhammad saw this as an area through which he was fleeing from something terrible. Before him, early Christians fleeing persecution from Rome settled here and created frescoe-rich churches and monasteries throughout the valleys.

He was on the Silk Road and it could lead him to the fresh life his father had described. Muhammad was also streetwise enough to know that drugs smugglers nowadays used this same route. Seljuk Turks had built respites for camel caravans travelling the route. These and the caves were chiselled into the tufa rock creating the underground settlements once used to escape the attentions of invaders.

Muhammad knew that he should use some of his money to take a train for rest of his journey across Turkey to Istanbul, which he perceived as one of the big cities of the West. His father had always encouraged him to speak English and he was able to buy the ticket from a hotel ticketing source. The concierge was used to handling strange requests and didn't seem at all phased that a 16-year-old Iraqi was travelling the length of Turkey unaccompanied.

There was only a train every two days, but fortune on his part meant that Muhammad could catch a train later the same day. It was a two-part journey and Muhammad was travelling in unreserved seating in the lowest class on the train. He didn't care. His main objective now was to get to somewhere large and anonymous. Istanbul was his steppingstone for this. In the area around Narli, although two countries away from his native Iraq, he could still understand the language surprisingly well. A part of the old Ottoman Empire and the dialects had survived.

Muhammad moved to the station and looked for where the train would appear. To his surprise, it was already in place at the platform, some two hours before departure. It was being stocked with water, drinks and snacks for the journey. He decided to see if he could get on board and found that they locked the doors, except by the area where items were being placed on board. He snuck on and found a seat. There were no warnings it was reserved, and he sat comfortably, using the small bag as a pillow for his head.

An hour later he was disturbed and awoken by another three people moving in this area of the train. They were foreigners talking in English, though he did not know where they were from. They were talking fast, but he could understand most of what they were saying. He noticed their short haircuts and wondered if they were military. One of them looked at him now he appeared awake.

"Isalaam Aleekum," said one of the British to Muhammad.

"Wa aleekum isalaam," replied Muhammad, automatically.

Muhammad realised from the look of the three travellers, that their language was limited to hello and welcome, so he switched into English.

"I go to Istanbul, this part of the train is correct, Yes?".

The three travellers smiled, "Yes, this is the right part of the train. We are also going to Istanbul, then flying back to England".

They smiled. Muhammad smiled back. These looked as if they would be trouble free companions. Muhammad noticed they had high technology phones and music equipment, expensive looking backpacks and stylish clothing. He decided they were wealthy and that the money and goods which he had would not be of much interest to people as wealthy as these three.

One of them offered him a can of drink - Coca Cola. He took it with some ceremony and watched as the three of them all took cans, clicked them open and began drinking. He had been sparing with water for the last three weeks and this was some contrast.

Another half an hour and the train lurched out of the station. There had been a lot of commotion with items being loaded and last-minute retail opportunities for bottled water, Turkish coffee in small paper cups served through the windows of the train and even some large cases being fed in through the windows instead of via the doors. Muhammad sat with the British people and wondered if he would get to Istanbul with nothing being stolen.

"What's your name?" asked one of the Brits. "My name is Robert, and here are Adam and Richard," he continued. "We have been seeing the beautiful countryside around Narli."

"I've been in the desert for the last three weeks," replied Muhammad, "It has been a long journey for me."

Muhammad described the village he had left and the long trip across difficult terrain to get to Syria and then across into Turkey. The area he had crossed was the western tip of Syria and also where the freight train line ran, and so he had taken an optimal route.

Robert looked at the other two Brits. "We know about that village. It has been in the news here." He asked, softly, "Did you know other people in the village?"

"My family were there, and many of my relatives and friends. I think I know someone murdered them," said

Muhammad, "I could see smoke and hear noises like gunshots as I left. I was already a long way from the village, but you are confirming something that I already knew."

Robert looked Muhammad in the eyes, "I'm sorry to be the one to tell you this."

"I'd known and have already had three weeks to grieve. Now I know I am alone and must make my own way. My father told me to find a fresh life."

Muhammad had just heard the news he had expected ever since he left the village. The first truck of soldiers was a vanguard for a larger group, and they were there to destroy what they saw as an oppositional force, based upon a different interpretation of religion. Muhammad's father had given Muhammad everything that the family possessed in order to help him make his escape. Almost certainly, his whole family were now slaughtered in the village and Muhammad was alone in the world.

"You are Kurdish?" asked Robert. Muhammad nodded, "Yes, it's where I live". As an Arab, Muhammad didn't see land borders in the same way as politicians. The land was for everyone. People should be able to live anywhere they wanted. He had just proved that by moving from Iraq, through Syria and into Turkey.

"Okay," said Robert, "I think it's better now that you keep your origins quiet unless an official asks you; you have some papers?"

Muhammad nodded, he knew his rucksack contained papers prepared many months earlier by his father. They were papers that should allow him to travel to many countries, as long as he had money.

"...So can you help me at all?", asked Muhammad, who at this stage didn't think he had anything to lose.

The three travellers looked at one another again. A local person well versed in desert-craft and with an understanding of the terrain and local dialects. This was a strong find for the travellers, as Muhammad spoke good English and did not have any other ties.

"We might be able to help," said Robert, as the train rattled onward through the orange landscape of Cappadocia. It would be another 750 kilometres before they reached Istanbul.

During his time in the desert, Muhammad had decided that Istanbul would be the start of his new life.

Istanbul, a real edge city, between East and West, spanning many different cultures. Part European and part in Asia, where it crosses the Bosphorus. The only metropolis in the world on two continents.

Istanbul, capital to three empires, the Romans, the Byzantine and the Ottomans. Then, after the establishment of the Republic of Turkey, the capital moved to Ankara although most Turks would still see Istanbul as the capital for all but government bureaucratic reasons.

It would be easy to get lost in Istanbul. Easy to find something to do. A way to make some money. Muhammad didn't mind starting low. He thought he had enough cash to get started, although the money from his father seemed to be American money. He would need to be careful so that people did not think he had stolen it.

But now, on the train, Muhammad had been given a new proposition by the three people on the train. Employment in return for a place to stay and some proper paperwork.

The work involved him travelling with them back into desert areas, providing translation, cultural references and access to locals. For Muhammad, the thought of a safe place, some cash and proper papers made a very compelling option for Muhammad. In this terrible situation he had found a good route.

"A bird in the hand is worth ten in the tree," he thought, remembering the Arab proverb.

So right there on the train, Muhammad had agreed to work with these three British military people and would accompany them to the British Embassy in Istanbul.

Muhammad knew that he was getting involved with something that may make him take sides, but there had been such terror in his own country that siding with people opposed to what had happened made sense.

At the embassy, the three travellers showed passes. Robert spent several minutes explaining the purpose of bringing Muhammad along. Muhammad could see that Robert wielded considerable influence. Muhammad was admitted to the embassy but taken to a separate area, where he was told they would question him before they would allow him regain contact with the others.

The room was pleasant enough, upstairs, in a separate block from the main buildings. There were guard dogs on the ground floor and armed militia inside and in most of the corridors.

Muhammad was offered fruit and drink and then after about twenty minutes someone came to ask him questions. he noticed that Robert, from the journey was also present, although now in fresh clothing and looked somewhat smarter than he had done on the train.

"It will be fine," said Robert, "Just tell them what you told us."

Muhammad thought for a minute in case this was some kind of trick but decided that it was safer to follow the instructions. He again explained his story and the route he had taken. His description was easy and unlaboured, because everything in it was very real and true. His questioners could see that too.

It did not take long for Muhammad to be provided with temporary accommodation in Istanbul and a small allowance, provided by Her Majesty's Government.

Muhammad had then been introduced to the work of Robert, Douglas and others. From the embassy, they were all trained for other more specialized duties and needed ways into and out of Syria, Iraq and Iran.

Muhammad became a guide and a translator for them and helped with missions which had a semi-military nature. Muhammad was happy to co-operate and considered the work of the UK Government to be a way that he could get back at the people who had destroyed his village.

Over the next few years his bitterness dulled, and in the same period the loyalty to his UK friends increased. Robert Alton, the first person he had met on that train rose through the ranks within the Government group and was soon a senior player, with Muhammad as a loyal supporter.

Lambeth Walk

Robert Alton was standing by Lambeth Bridge as Muhammad and Douglas approached.

"Coffee?" asked Robert Alton.

"Water, maybe," smiled Muhammad.

Doug nodded. "You too, Robert? I'll get them, let's find a quiet spot." He walked towards the small coffee shop perched on the edge of a jetty by the Thames.

"It's odd, even the television spy series use this stretch of the river," said Muhammad.

"I know," said Robert Alton, "I think it's also because they can get the Houses of Parliament into the background."

"So why aren't there lots of microphones and surveillance cameras around here?"

"Oh, there are. And not just ours. Even the juice bar over there is wired up. But we'll walk along the road over there in a minute. It's out of any practical range. And, after all, we are only talking about the next all-Department meeting."

Doug returned with three bottles of water.

"Okay, let's go."

They turned from the walk alongside the Thames back onto a busy main road.

"I wanted this to be away from normal recording because I think we may have a loose tongue somewhere inside the Department," said Robert. "I need people I can trust on this."

He turned to face Doug and Muhammad. "Look, Karen has been killed. It looks like she was run down on a package exchange mission. I've checked through her files. She'd insulated the mission using a stringer to do the exchange. There's no name on file."

"What was the mission about?" asked Doug.

"It's linked to a threat we received about some terrorist movements in London and Frankfurt. The package that was being moved was linked in some way. I'm going to go 'upstairs' to try to get more information."

"What was in the package?" asked Muhammad.

"We don't know. We just know that it was supposed to be of a size that a single operative could collect and move in the back of a car."

"Could it have been a bomb?" asked Muhammad.

"Bomb, money, drugs; we just don't know. The truck carrying the package was destroyed. Blown up by a missile from a helicopter."

"What?" said Doug, "This isn't in mission reports. All it said something about Karen in a road traffic accident in Cairo."

"I know," said Alton, "It has been given a cover story. It was all very messy. Karen was shot down in a cafe. Before that, the helicopter that destroyed the truck was blown up by a surface to air. The stringer guy running pickup has disappeared. It's a mess. The whole trail is dead."

"That's where you come in," said Alton. "We need to get on top of this. Find the stringer. Bring him in."

"What about the people operating with Karen?" asked Muhammad, "She would have a team with her."

"She did, but it's no good," said Alton, "After the shooting, they went into hiding. There were two of them.

One's now back here in London, the other is still in Cairo. They are good people. The one in Cairo says that there is a rumour that the helicopter was Israeli."

"Shit," said Doug. "That would put the cat among the pigeons".

"Yes, and now we must seek a white dove of peace," continued Alton. "This could already be a major incident if the word gets out that the Israelis were flying missions into Egypt."

"Not one for us though?" questioned Doug.

"Not directly," answered Alton, "Although if the U.K. involvement is discovered it would change things. More importantly, there's what this all means, linked back to the terror threat. I think Karen stumbled into something much bigger than we expected."

"And it does create a useful trail for us?" said Muhammad. "If the Israelis were prepared to send an unauthorised gunship chopper into Egypt, then they must know something about the truck or it's package?"

"My thoughts, too," said Alton. "We will need a small team that can operate away from base for this. There seems to be a leak. And it seems to be cross border too. If it's as sloppy as it appears then the smugglers, terrorists or whatever they are know what is going on too."

Robert Alton looked at Muhammad and Doug carefully, "You know this needs total discretion. This situation is a Category One threat".

Muhammad and Doug nodded.

"We'll go external," said Doug. "It will be easier if you can give us another cover investigation. That way we can be off-grid but with a reason."

"Use something that won't involve too many other people. How about that gas fracking security probe up north?" suggested Alton.

"Perfect," said Doug, "Miles of fields and hills to investigate based upon a security rumour."

"I'll up its security level too, so that access to what is happening becomes more limited," said Alton, "…And Muhammad, your cover story is because we suspect parallels with something that has happened in the middle east."

They had arrived in an area close to another busy south London traffic intersection.

"There's someone else I'm going to meet about this later this afternoon. Someone I shouldn't really be talking to. I'll let you know how I get on.

The Square

"We should split up here; Gentlemen, a pleasure," said Alton, "Oh, and remember - only communicate to me in person on this and all meetings off site."

Ed Adams

TWO WEEKS EARLIER

The Pentagon

*I think it makes people in the Pentagon kind of nervous
to know that chemical agents and environmental factors
could cause so much damage
in terms of what may happen in the future.*

Bernie Sanders

Washington Alert

When the first news of the terrorist plans reached the National Security Agency in Washington and GCHQ in the United Kingdom, they conducted a trawl to find senior ranking experts who could interpret what was happening.

They had called Robert Alton for this reason. He had also asked to involve Muhammad. There had been ripples of dissent from command office, but Robert was by now very senior and vouched for Muhammad's integrity.

Muhammad had spent ten years in loyal service, initially overseas in Turkey, but then since he was 26, spending time in the UK in some of the more sensitive control and command centres related to understanding Middle Eastern motives. Muhammad knew his way around now and at 28 years old was fit and self-confident. He had shown unwavering support for Robert since they had met and had been involved in exercises which spanned the continents and countries around the middle east.

The news from GCHQ gave Karen and Muhammad a lot to work on. They had a sense that there was a serious attempt being made to do something on a large scale to cripple London and other UK centres.

"Why don't we announce something?" asked Muhammad, already aware of the protocol.

"We can't," replied Karen, "Two main reasons; it would create widespread panic, and this can create further problems of its own and second, it is better that the terrorist doesn't know we are on to them as we close in."

The plan was now to determine and triangulate the sources and reliability of the information about the plot. Muhammad would send out probes via the internet and through the cellular network, to see if there was further information.

Muhammad also now had a strong network, so he was sure that if there was news, he would stand a good chance to find it.

Muhammad's problem with the briefing from Karen and Robert was that he had no idea what he was looking for. It was some kind of plot, involved London (or maybe Frankfurt) and was terrorist led, by people from the Middle East. Next stop was Government Communication Head Quarters (GCHQ-Cheltenham), to see whether there was any more concrete intelligence to help him in his task.

Muhammad didn't have the top-level security clearance and needed someone who could help him with this part of the activity. Because of Muhammad's background, he was still regarded as an outsider by some parts of the British security fraternity and so full clearance was all but impossible.

He called Karen and asked for her help. She agreed and together they called GCHQ to ask about other intercepts and links with other significant events.

They were patched through to a Commander Simpson from GCHQ, who asked a series of detailed security clearance questions before he was prepared to proceed any further. They were on a top secured line between their headquarters and GCHQ and Karen had Level 1 clearance. Commander Simpson was satisfied with this and relaxed as he prepared to answer questions.

"Here's what we have," he began. "some intercepts from Iran and Pakistan suggested that there was an increase of information flow related to the geography of parts of Central London around Parliament Square and Whitehall and also around the Western part of Frankfurt in the financial district."

"We have been tracing the calls and some of the calls have been to call boxes in West London, mainly around the

Paddington area". Then we picked up satellite phone calls, also from West London, which seemed to link to the same thing."

"We think there is a cell operating in London and that they have acquired some nuclear or chemical/biological agents which they intend to use in an attack. For the last couple of weeks, we have been trying to identify if there has been any major theft of loss of materials. That's when we discovered a cover-up that has been operating at CTL."

"CTL?" queried Karen, "what is that?"

"CTL is Chemical Testing Labs, it is part of Porton Down," continued Commander Simpson, "They test new and specialised chemical and biological agents, whether UK, US or originated from other areas. Two weeks ago, a consignment of tubes containing a new compound going by the name Crylo-37 was diverted en route to a testing suite and has not been recovered. It is believed to still be inside the complex but has not been located. This is very irregular, and we are holding a full investigation. Crylo-37A is a neuro toxin antidote for one of the deadliest nerve toxins identified. The test tubes are not normal glass ones. They are special titanium containers with injection capabilities. The antidote is to be used against a severe form of nerve agent."

"So, we have a terrorist alert and a mysterious disappearance of nerve agent antidote? both within a two week timeframe?", queried Karen, "This is rather a large co-incidence?"

"Precisely", said Commander Simpson, "That's why we have alerted your organisation as well as a few other Agencies, but we are still keeping this Strictly Confidential. We have not told press or public and even kept this from all except the Defence Secretary, Bernard Driscoll. It's the same intel with the US and Germany at the moment, and with Germany, they know about the terrorist alert but not the nerve agent. We had to tell the Americans because the original nerve agent compound was American, and they would wonder what had happened to it."

"I know we are not supposed to make assumptions", said Karen, "but this is too much of a co-incidence. Is there any chance that the tubes will still be found inside CTL?"

"It's unlikely", replied Commander Simpson, "The individual tubes have activated RFID within the facility, which means every cylinder can be pin-pointed by radio waves to within a few centimetres. Away from the facility, the RFID needs specialised equipment to track it, because of its short range.

"The more dangerous compounds (like the actual nerve agents) also have an outer container which includes satellite tracking. They are set up as binary too, which means they have to be activated and mixed together by a digital code, before they become lethal.

The Square

"The tracker transmitter used in the container for the toxin tubes has to be switched on. It uses composite technologies. A radio transmission and a special circuit which made it appear as an internet node similar to a web site. This precaution means that it, like any other highly valuable cargo could be traced without giving away that it was special.

To start the signalling a special code sequence is needed which is a hardware address wired into the tracker.

These gadgets are a fairly new technology and only used in two main areas : specialised weaponry and for extremely high-risk items such as nuclear and highly toxic chemical components that were on the move.

The hardware address was kept under secure access control. You'll have to get the address codes from the Defence Secretary.

"Do you have a picture of one of the canisters and one of the antidote tubes?", asked Karen, A screen flicked on in the room and a back projection appeared showing a couple of pictures. One looked like a bomb or missile and the other a machined metallic cylinder with a complex top mechanism.

"Wow", said Muhammad, "That's some cylinder and some test tube".

"Yes", said Commander Simpson, "We don't want them to be breakable or for just anyone to be able to hack into what is a massively secret payload".

"You are talking about these as if they are bombs", responded Karen.

"The nerve agent canisters are", replied Commander Simpson.

"A single canister, diffused into the air, could have a devastating effect upon a population of 50 to 100 thousand, depending on wind conditions. The effective life of the agent compound is around 24 hours - a so called 'short spike' - and that is why it is supposed to be such an effective but deadly compound. Normal troops can re-enter an area where it has been deployed soon after its use."

"But this is totally illegal and breaks every rule of warfare," said Karen.

"Correct," replied Simpson, "Unfortunately, it cannot be un-invented and that is why it is being examined at present, to understand its weaknesses and to provide emergency procedures should it ever be deployed. The nerve agent canisters are truly Weapon of Mass Destruction."

"And part of the reason it is being examined at Porton Down is to check the weapon's footprint and frailties. We need to be able to tell when it has been used, like the detection of the way that Saddam Hussein deployed chemicals.

"Is this after the fact?" asked Karen.

"It kind of is," replied Simpson, "But we have little choice in these troubled times, and failing to have any response whatsoever would be criticised just as heavily."

"So, we now have a lethal nerve toxin, probably in the hands of terrorists and possible threats on London and Frankfurt," continued Karen.

"And enough toxin in circulation to damage all of the major population centres of the United Kingdom," added Commander Simpson, "Although they seem to have stolen the antidote as well."

Muhammad and Karen made their way to Robert Alston's office to provide him a full update. He listened to their news and realised they now had a dead-end, since the containers had gone invisible.

"Muhammad, do you think you have enough to make some enquiries?"

Muhammad nodded. He was well-connected. Since spending time in the United Kingdom he had learnt a lot and acted well. He had access to local Mosque communities and through his attendance at varied group meetings, he had a strong access to what was happening in the London area. He admitted to himself that there was no word about the current situation anywhere in the community. No-one had talked about chemical plots, or the arrival of any special activists from overseas.

Muhammad would spend time searching for information and try to seed some rumours which could cause something to surface. He decided that an announcement about a suspected terrorist cell in Central London would be a good way to shake some information from the trees. He knew a few contacts where the word could be put out and would create a desired amount of gossip.

"I'm on to it," said Muhammad as he walked towards the door of the room.

Hoxton

Jake was just leaving the offices of 'The Triangle' for the evening. It was in the trendy part of Hoxton, not far from the well-known Hoxton Square, which had its own bustle every evening.

When Jake had stated the company with Clare and Bigsy, they had decided it needed a base in London. They had come into some serious money as a result of a previous escapade and the advice they received made them think it wise to create a proper base for whatever they decided to do next.

Hoxton emerged as the first choice for a couple of reasons.

Firstly, it was near enough to the centre of London and in an area generally considered to be quite cutting edge.

Secondly, they had been told by Richard their estate agent friend, that Hoxton was one of the areas where property prices were moving up the fastest. Richard had been right and despite the general economic conditions, almost from the time that they acquired the property they had seen its value soar.

The Triangle had come about after a grisly set of events where one of Jake's friends had been murdered. They had been caught up in the aftermath, befriended a solitary American known as Chuck Manners and through lengthy series of events had eventually collected a sizeable amount of cash.

They all knew that the origins of the original funds were dubious, but that there was no practical way to declare or hand in the money without putting themselves in danger.

Instead, they had walked away with enough funds to do what they wanted and had set up the Triangle business as a convincing front for whatever they decided to do next.

The company was a media organisation with a small investigatory business on the side. It fitted well with Jake's interest in journalism, Bigsy's clever ways of working with technology and Clare's grasp of media and photography. They had skills for certain types of activity, although there was little way to publicise the more fringe aspects of their existence.

Jake had been pleased to get the call from Clare about their mutual friend Christina.

The Square

"Hi Clare, where are you right now?"

"Doing fine, Jake, and I was on my way over to meet Christina, I thought I'd call you about that little meeting Christina and I had with the promoters. Looks like there may be a gig."

"Sounds great" said Jake,

"Yes, there's a series of concerts in the summer and they are keen to get Christina as the support act. We're just back from the meeting and headed across to the South Bank, do you fancy a drink?"

Jake nodded as he spoke into his phone. "Sure thing, where?"

"How about the Cafe at the BFI? We can watch the world while we chat?" Clare smiled to Christina - they would share their story with Jake over a bottle of wine.

Jake finished his call, just as another message appeared on the phone. A text message.

A blast from the past, after 18 months, it was a message from Chuck Manners. Jake tensed. It wouldn't be a call to see how he was doing. There must be more to it.

The message was characteristically short and obtuse.

"Hi Jake, I'll need to meet you, will call later. Chuck."

Jake tapped in two letters and replied.

"OK," he said.

Whatever it was that Chuck wanted, Jake knew this would be no idle request.

Politician

Hey now, baby
Get into my big black car
I want to just show you
What my politics are

Jack Bruce / Pete Brown

Defence Secretary

Robert Alton was in his office at SI6. He had been unsuccessful at speaking to the Bernard Driscoll, the blustery Defence Secretary.

Given the current situation, he was surprised by the lack of contact. It could only mean that the Defence Secretary already knew something about the situation and maybe had another team working on it.

Alton decided that a personal appearance would be the next stage and he would need to get some answers to serious questions.

Robert Alton made a direct visit to the Defence Secretary. The Defence Secretary had potent powers within the United Kingdom reaching into policing, crime reduction, counter-terrorism, immigration, asylum and citizenship as well as the related topics of identity cards and passports.

A situation involving terrorism within the United Kingdom using nerve agent weapons should be high on his priority list, yet Alton seemed to sense that there was a muting of interest in the topic.

"Hello Robert," began Defence Secretary Bernard Driscoll, "To what do I owe this pleasure?" His eyes sparkled with interest but if he knew about the terrorist incident, he was not giving much away.

"It's about the alert," explained Robert, "We think this one is real."

"Ah, the terrorist alert in London... and / or Frankfurt?" replied Driscoll, "We have been watching this one, but don't think it is serious. We have between ten and thirty alerts active on average and most of them are rather feeble-minded and some are even pranks which do just waste our resources."

"A couple of months ago we had a Channel Tunnel alert which was extremely plausible but turned out to be animal rights activists on some kind of crusade about foxes."

"We think this is being covered up from inside", said Alton, "that people even from your areas are involved and are hiding their tracks.

"I've already been looking into it, let's say that there's some vested interests in this one" replied Driscoll, waving his hands in front of Alton.

"What do you mean?" asked Alton.

"Another government or two could be very embarrassed"

"What, the Germans?"

"...No, not the Germans." His hands continued to have a life of their own, " Look, this is very delicate. There are some international relations at stake. It overstates the threat, although we do wish to get back a certain consignment."

"Do you want us to stop what we are doing?" asked Alton, "Things could get out of hand." Alton was amused to see that his last phrase had temporarily halted the wilder flourishes from Driscoll.

"No, continue to do what you do. It will arouse the least suspicion. I don't think you will find anything though," answered Driscoll.

"Look, Defence Secretary, if I find anything, I will inform you. I will also need some freedom to act on this one."

"Robert, take all the freedom you need," smiled Driscoll, "but be careful not to upset any of our big friends."

The Square

Alton shook Driscoll's hand, and patted him on the right shoulder. Then Alton took his leave.

It had been a very short meeting but Robert had achieved his primary objective. He had attached a small bug with a short-range transmitter. Now he could hear what Driscoll was doing. He walked back to the outer lobby of the building, where he could pick up his mobile phone, which he had been asked to hand in before visiting the Defence Secretary. Some would think this unusual, but there were so many ways to infiltrate using cell-phones that he was not at all surprised at the tightening of security.

Back outside, he flipped his phone on and dialled a special number. Sure enough, he could hear some sounds from Driscoll's office and then he heard Driscoll making a call on a secure link to someone else.

"Avi," he heard, "There have been people around to check what has been happening. Someone is creating a leak. You need to block it".

Robert could not hear the other end of the call. "Yes, yes...I told them that there was nothing unusual and that this alert was commonplace...You need to locate the missing pieces and have them destroyed...We have set up tracking...The trackers for the nerve agent and the antidotes have both been activated...This is still need to know...I cannot stay on this connection any longer."

Robert had listened intently during the call and left the listening device open now. He wondered if Driscoll would make further calls but instead, he heard Driscoll getting ready to leave the office. The type of listening device used by Robert had two major drawbacks. The first was because of its small size it only had a very short battery life. The second was that its range was limited to 500 metres and through walls and metal the range was even more limited. If Driscoll went out now, the device would have no further use. The design of the unit was small pin that looked like a piece from lady's jewellery, It would not stand close scrutiny, but had a high chance that if discovered would be assumed to be a lost item rather than a bug.

In the meantime, Robert now had a name. Not much to go on, but the name was Avi.

Robert called Dorothy, "I've some more investigation for you," he continued, "I'm looking for someone named Avi?"

"Do you mean Avi Abner?", replied Dorothy immediately, "Head of the Israeli Intelligence Agency here in London?"

Robert nearly kicked himself that he had not thought of this. "Dorothy, thank you!" he continued. In a moment Dorothy had short-circuited something which could have been a long and protracted search, to probably the right answer based upon her own encyclopaedic knowledge.

"In that case, Dorothy, Please can you help me create a reason for a short term meeting with Mr Abner?"

"How about lapsed renewal of diplomatic passes, leading to ejection of two or three of his people if not dealt with immediately? We can claim it was an error after the meeting!"

"Perfect!" replied Robert. He knew he was getting into something very clandestine now. The Israeli Intelligence Agency was the polite name for the organisation usually referred to as Mossad. They were involved with counter terrorism and covert activities and had been linked with many rumours including forged British passports found in grocery bags, letter bombings, several allegations about assassinations including of the Canadian involved with the Iraqi super-gun and failed attempts such as a poison attempt on a senior Jordanian official.

Robert prepared himself for what he knew would be a tough session and he knew that Mossad would see straight through any renewed diplomatic passes ruse and realise that they were being approached about something else. Dorothy called back within ten minutes.

"You have a meeting," she said, "It's going to be on Westminster Bridge, in two hours, at four pm". Robert was impressed. Dorothy knew a lot of people and there was another layer of 'fixing' involved in getting meetings.

Robert was a senior official and so his own 'label' got a few doors opened, but Dorothy needed to know how to play the game to get things set up as fast as this. It suggested that there was something big in play and that the Israelis were willing to assist.

Westminster Bridge

Robert Alton stayed away from his office until his next meeting. He would take a taxi, then double back on the tube. His next meeting was very close, but he would take a circuitous route.

At the appointed time he was walking across Westminster Bridge.

"Oh, how the seasons change," said a deep and friendly voice behind him. He turned to see an over-coated, bearded short man with a dark hat. He was smiling and caught up to walk alongside Robert.

"Avi! It has been a while! Too long, probably."

"Robert - Too long, yes. And the last time was when we were talking about those bus bombs in Tel Aviv. We should find reasons to get together that are pleasant. To talk about times in Oxford."

Avi Abner shook hands and then patted Robert on the back.

"No Avi, I'm not wired up, I'm alone and this is off grid," said Alton.

"Desperate times," answered Avi.

"Desperate measures," replied Alton. He paused and looked Avi in the eye. He was pleased to see Avi, despite the vicious power that he wielded.

"Avi, We know about the truck. The one crossing the desert."

"There are a lot of deserts," said Avi, "...and a lot of trucks, come to that."

They had walked south across Westminster Bridge. Ahead was a large hotel.

Avi continued, "Let's go inside, we can get a coffee or something. And if I knew what was being targeted, what reason would I have to tell you? We could both find ourselves in a lot of trouble."

"I think we are already both in a lot of possible trouble over this one," replied Alton.

"Assurances," said Avi, "Assurances. If I tell you more about this, you'll be implicated and there's no easy way back. I need your assurance that you will play this close. And that you'll limit any damage to Israel and me."

"I'm already off-grid for this," said Alton, "I'm running this covertly. You have my assurance this is between the two of us."

They were on an escalator to the first floor, where there was a coffee area. They sat in a quiet area, with a large plate-glass window view back across the bridge towards the Big Ben clock tower.

"Frankly, I think we have a leak," said Alton, "That's why I'm running this quietly."

"I know you have a leak. That's what caused this situation in the first place," said Avi.

"Okay, you'd better explain."

Avi started, "Let's hypothesize that there is a threat. A threat to the UK and maybe to Germany. And let's say it is terrorist inspired. Maybe the British don't know enough to stop them. Perhaps someone else knows more. Perhaps someone else can stop them in a way that doesn't implicate the British."

"Now why would anyone want to do that?" asked Robert.

"Let's consider; you might think there are some people that don't see eye to eye with what might be an Arab terrorist. But, and here's the very sensitive part, perhaps the terrorists would use something that they gained from another country, and perhaps they had got it illegally."

Robert's mind raced. "What? I still don't know what we are dealing with here. Is it something that Israel produced?"

Avi continued, "It's good that you work this out rather than me telling you. Let's assume that a friendly power wanted to show the United Kingdom some materials it had constructed. Let's say that the materials were an inconvenience to the friendly power, and they wanted know the best and most permanent methods of destruction."

"Perhaps the United Kingdom was more specialised in the ways to handle such troublesome substances. But maybe somehow the substance was intercepted in transit."

"What, it was stolen?" asked Alton.

"Fortunately, the cylinder included a tracking device which was activated to determine that the substance had been moved."

Alton responded, "I see. This would create something of a predicament for the British Government and for the other friendly power. I assume they expected the consignment to get to the United Kingdom without explicit paperwork?"

Avi nodded, "You still have excellent powers of deduction."

Alton interrupted, "Avi, you will need to be more specific with me if you expect me to help with this. I've already lost a good agent in the field, and our other trails are dead. We don't know what we are looking for."

The coffee arrived, and Avi immediately paid the waitress. He waited until she had walked away before continuing.

"Okay. You seem to have worked out part of this, anyway. The truck contains toxins. They were supposed to be taken to Porton Down in the UK for disposal. Someone intercepted their route and stole the cylinders. We think the route was leaked from the UK, but can't prove it."

"Why take the toxin all the way from Israel to the UK to destroy it?" asked Alton.

"You know how these things work. It would all be destroyed except for a 'file sample' which Porton Down would keep for a rainy day.

"But why ship so much?"

"It's regenerative and the only way to be sure is with the technology that they have in Porton Down. Look - it was a weaponised tertiary toxin."

"Tertiary?" asked Alton. "I know about binaries, what's a tertiary?"

"Like a binary, there's two parts to activate it. The third part is an antidote. It can neutralise the toxin but also stop its effects. The part in the desert was the bulk half of the binary. A small reactive agent is added to make it live. Another different agent can neutralise it."

Avi looked at Alton. "I can make this all go away, if I have the precision tracker codes. I'll arrange a strike, and then only the antidote will be out there. That's no use without the main toxin."

Avi continued, "This is also time critical. At the moment the cylinders are still in the middle east, although they have already moved from the original holding location. Another day and they will have worked out how to move it to somewhere that may be much harder to strike."

"Okay, so suppose I can get the code. How would this work?" asked Alton.

"Detached. I can arrange everything. Swift, clinical. No British implications."

"What about Israel?"

"No, no Israeli implications either. It will look like mercenaries.

"Give me a little while to find out about this," said Alton. "And is there a secure private way that I can reach you?"

"Take this," said Avi. He handed Alton a cellphone. It looked well-used.

"Old school. Sometimes it's still the best way. It's from a secondhand shop and has been re-chipped. It's got a full charge. These old phones stay charged for days. Don't use it for anything else and throw it away when we are done," said Avi.

"Avi - it's been interesting," said Alton.

"Don't forget, this is urgent," replied Avi, "and afterwards we really should have a proper lunch together, maybe in Oxford?"

Robert Alton shook Avi's hand and turned to leave the hotel's coffee bar. He would pick up a taxi from the front of the hotel, back to SI6. He had a busy afternoon ahead briefing Karen on her visit to Egypt.

Thames House

Robert Alton arrived back at Thames House. The journey by taxi had taken about fifteen minutes, which was a consequence of the amount of traffic in Central London. He re-entered the secure area and made his way to his office. His assistant, Dorothy, was waiting.

"I have the codes," Dorothy said, "from an excellent source - the Defence Secretary."

"Codes?" repeated Robert, "I was expecting one."

Alton considered. Defence Secretary Bernard Driscoll must be rattled to have sent the codes through in this way. Maybe he was looking for a scapegoat.

"There are two sets", said Dorothy, "And they were requested together- One set comprises an arm and a disarm protocol. The other set starts a precision tracker. They are both listed as munitions.

The Square

Alton thought again, why would Driscoll send two sets of codes across, when he'd only asked for one? Driscoll knew more about this situation than he was letting on.

Dorothy continued, "I will hand them to you, you must then re-encrypt them and we must then destroy the paper where I have written the information."

Robert knew this protocol and retrieved a paperback from his pocket. This ancient process was to be the source of his encryption.

Digital security had superseded arcane processes with books and cyphers, yet Alton knew the real story.

The digital codes were easier to break. Not by any normal person, but by the Americans.

They had persuaded everyone that digital was stronger, but what it did was ensure that encrypted codes were more visible on the internet.

As for cracking the codes, the irony of the American system was that it forbade the use of certain types of cryptography. In effect, the codes had to be crackable.

Alton knew that his use of a paperback book and a sequence of randomised letters would be a stronger code than anything using regular digital encryption. It was so strong that even a different imprint of the book would give a different result.

He looked at the code and wrote a different sequence onto a fresh piece of paper, referring all the time to the paperback.

"These codes have never been stored anywhere electronic?" asked Robert.

"Correct" said Dorothy, "Nor been discussed on any phone line. This is absolute Level 5 material now."

They both smiled at the rather odd title for Level Five Security - Beyond Top Secret it was referred to as 'Cosmic Top Secret' - someone in NATO had decided to have a little joke the day that term was invented.

He was using the paperback as a long cipher encryption key for his work.

"Dorothy, thank you again," he said as he finished the sequence and the two of them tore the original paper into insignificant pieces and then set fire to it in a small container designed for this purpose. At the end Dorothy added a small container of chemical to the remnants which were, by this time, unrecognisable.

"You now have the only copy of the codes, except for the Defence Realm Registry and your version is encrypted using a one time code." Robert knew the protocol. He now had to decide whether to give the information to Avi.

The Square

"Let me make the call to my associate," he said to Dorothy. There was no point in telling Dorothy more than she needed to know. If this came out, Dorothy would be questioned. She understood the advantages of 'need to know' basis in such circumstances.

Robert left the building again. He didn't want more than necessary to be captured in the unremitting cameras of Thames House. He phoned Avi on the special phone Avi had provided.

"I will be on a 452 bus south of Chelsea Bridge in one hour," he said.

"See you", said Avi.

Robert made his way to Sloane Square in west London, around ten minutes by foot from Chelsea Bridge. He would wait here until the allotted time and then catch the bus to the bridge. The bus service was frequent, more than one every ten minutes. He waited until around five minutes to six, hopped onto a bus and climbed upstairs. Here he had a suitable vantage point from the front windows.

A few minutes later the bus was crossing the bridge over the Thames with the tall chimneys of Battersea Power Station off to the left-hand side. Sure enough, as the bus stopped over the bridge, Avi climbed on board and made his way to the seat behind Robert.

"It's here," said Robert, and pointed to an envelope, which contained the encrypted codes.

"Thank you", said Avi. You will need something else, replied Robert.

"Aha, the key", responded Avi, "When?"

"Once I am away from this bus," replied Robert.

"Of course," said Avi.

Robert smiled and stood to exit the bus.

"I'll call you in a minute, stay on the bus," said Robert.

He exited and as the bus drove away he called Avi to explain where he had hidden the paperback on the bus.

It was behind a seat at the other end of the upper deck. With the encrypted code and the book as a key, Avi would be able to translate the code back for his purposes.

Avi smiled as he located the book. It was a simple substitution cipher to get the code. Easy to decode with the book, impossible to crack without. He now had not just one code, but to his surprise he now had two codes.

Walk like an Egyptian

All the bazaar men by the Nile
They got the money on a bet
Gold crocodiles (oh way oh)
They snap their teeth on your cigarette

Foreign types with the hookah pipes say
Way oh way oh, way oh way oh
Walk like an Egyptian

Bangles/ Liam Hillard Sternberg

Coded binary

Karen Martin was already waiting in Robert Alton's office. She had taken the call from Dorothy and, realising its importance, come straight across.

"Karen, you know the Egyptian situation," said Alton.

Karen nodded, "What is this about?" she asked.

"We've some stolen equipment to neutralise," explained Alton.

"It's a neurotoxin. Multiple containers. They are worth a lot to bad people. We've got to disable them."

Alton was taking no chances. He knew Avi Abner was on to the case, but he would also run a mission of his own, to create a similar outcome, which would at least be the neutralisation of the nerve agent.

"Disable them? And how do we do that?" asked Karen.

"The neurotoxin is a coded binary. We can use shutdown codes to neutralise it. That will render it useless. The neurotoxin will self-clean."

Alton decided he would keep Avi's role and the Israeli part out of his explanation.

" Take a stringer and use the stringer to intercept a truck, which will cross the desert. We can give you the co-ordinates of the truck because its cargo will be sending out a tracker signal.

"Your stringer has two jobs.

"He needs to hand over codes held in an electronically locked briefcase. In return, the stringer should also receive a bag back."

"What happens then?" asked Karen.

"We'll need to set the codes on the devices, and they will disarm."

"What about the codes to re-arm them?"

Karen realised that there would be a second set of codes to override the actions of the first set. In effect an Arm and Disarm set, with the material in transit in the disarmed state.

"Agreed, there are some codes, but we don't need them for this exercise. Once we've disarmed the consignments, they can't be restarted in any case. Disarm is a polite word for 'destroy'"

"That sound simple enough," said Karen, "What is the problem with it? Is it 'hot' or something?"

"Very hot," answered Alton, "They are likely to be pursued. Your job is to wait in Cairo for the return of the stringer."

"Will the stringer be at risk from the destruction codes?" asked Karen.

"No, the cylinders contain internal chemicals which are released to do their work," Answered Alton.

"When your stringer returns, we know that we have passed the disarm codes to the truck. Then they will need to be actioned by the driver."

"So, the driver is one of ours too?" asked Karen.

"I hope so," answered Alton.

Firepower

Avi was an experienced operative, and the code provided by Robert Alton was easy to decipher once he had the paperback book.

The code was the sequence needed to enable and locate the transmitters for the two consignments.

He had everything he needed to activate a plan to get the consignment destroyed. He would use military firepower for this and particularly large conventional weaponry to create such a fireball that nothing would survive.

There was a slight risk of toxic escape, but with a large enough warhead he could be sure that the toxins with their short half-life would be annihilated.

Avi decided that this mission was so delicate that he would supervise in person, from Israel. The people involved needed to be as few as possible and everyone needed to have it made clear just how secret this mission would be.

Avi decided to catch the plane that evening across to Tel Aviv. He could fly on El-Al and this would be a direct overnight to Ben Gurion Airport in Tel Aviv.

He headed first to his office, prepared some paperwork to speed his transit through the airport security systems ,and then arranged for a taxi to take him to London's Heathrow Airport. His use of his diplomatic status gave him a slightly faster and more pleasant route through the airport, when compared with many of the other travellers planning to fly to Israel.

It was a five-and-a-half-hour flight across most of Europe and then along the coast of the Mediterranean and down to the strife-torn area of Israel and its surrounding desert. Many years ago, a small group of Jewish families had moved from the overcrowded, insanitary and hostile Arab town of Jaffa to a selected desert spot which became Tel Aviv.

Avi could see lights of the city on the Mediterranean coast which had developed at great speed and brought with it some characteristics of an American city. Residents sometimes compared Tel Aviv to New York and in a short time, Tel Aviv had absorbed tens of thousands of refugees from Europe, Asia, Africa and South America and turned them into free citizens in their own homeland.

The Square

Above all, Tel Aviv appeared as a beach city; a broad expanse of fine sand extending over 6 miles along the seashore. City residents poured onto the beach for air, space and relaxation every weekend and at any opportunity during the day. The wide promenade runs for miles all the way from the port in north Tel Aviv to the old quarter of Jaffa which had become a popular waterside dining and leisure district of Tel Aviv. Although mentioned several times in the Bible and developed as Jerusalem's principal seaport, Jaffa gives little sense of its long history.

Only a small section of Old Jaffa remains today, its lanes and stairways cleaned up and restored beyond recognition and the squalid centre replaced by a park. Most of the town was built after Napoleon's destructive raid in 1799. Thus, the oldest port in the world (with all its trade long ago moved to Tel Aviv or Haifa) has become a mere district of a modern city.

Here, in the mid-morning, Avi Abner met with two members of the Israeli Air Force to discuss the interception of the trucks. The two men arrived in their civilian clothes, although both had military haircuts and wore dark aviator sunglasses. It was not so unusual to see military anywhere in Israel. Most people had completed compulsory military service, and guns on the street were commonplace.

"Shalom," began Avi, "Let me explain the situation. We have a security risk and need to take down a truck which will be in the desert. We need speed but also an ability to cope with a very rough terrain," he added.

"The contents of the trucks are lethal, and we must use a large amount of explosive to ensure that nothing survives," he added.

"We will have satellite tracking to help us locate the targets. We have co-ordinates and a real time feed. There is one thing though", he added.

"The desert in question is in Egypt".

The two members of the Israeli Air Force looked at each other and then back at Avi.

"Commander Abner", one started, "What you are describing is illegal. We could be shot down by the Egyptians or the Americans or anyone from a peace keeping force."

"This mission will be highly covert," continued Avi, "You will use an unmarked helicopter for the mission and because you have the exact co-ordinates and will be operating in the desert, the whole mission inside Egyptian airspace will be a matter of minutes".

"F15s can scramble in minutes " came the comment.

"You will have enough time and you will fly the helicopter as close to ground as possible. There will be a route which will protect you from radar and border controls. There will be a time window for you to operate. Let's just say the Egyptians owe us for something."

"When?" asked one of the pilots.

"Tomorrow, " answered Avi.

At 14:00 the next day, the two pilots were flying an electronically cloaked unmarked black Apache helicopter along the Egyptian border before encroaching into Egyptian military airspace at an altitude of 30 feet. The helicopter tracked terrain but showed no signs of being followed.

They locked on to a signal beacon ,which was moving slowly along a road. As they approached the target and their target acquisition system switched in, they elevated the helicopter to a safe firing height and then let loose a single high -powered missile towards the target. As it left the helicopter, they felt the recoil, but it was immediately interrupted by the sound from the targeting alert.

"We're lit up," said the pilot, "something has acquired us, I'm taking evasive action." At that moment their own missile hit the truck and the sky rocked with an explosion out of all expected proportion. They didn't have time to wonder what had happened because they were in the midst of their own programmed evasion.

The helicopter banked, jettisoned hot strips of metal to decoy the missile, but they could see on their radar that it was on a collision course. One second later the helicopter was struck and with a huge explosion the helicopter's world stopped and the simple physics of gravity took over. No survivors from the helicopter or the truck.

Driscoll

Defence Secretary Bernard Driscoll was worried.

He needed to handle the missing toxin situation from within the UK. It needed to be kept secret on account of the way the chemical agent was in the UK in the first place.

"I have some codes which may need to be intercepted," Driscoll had called the US operations room in the American Embassy in London. He was using the priority phone.

"Sure thing," said Colonel O'Malley, waving to others in his own facility to listen in, "How can we expedite this?"

O'Malley was an intermediary. He didn't really know the significance of the codes or the situation. But he could get them wired back to the NSA in Maryland and there would be fast action. Depending upon where the codes referenced would affect how the US processed them.

The codes were wired on a secure system to the USA, where the trackers were shown as deactivated, and the static markers were showing in an area of desert near to Riyadh, at a US Air Force base.

This was a fairly ideal situation, because it meant the consignments were currently being stored in an isolated area of desert. If a removal was to take place, then this would be a great location, away from built-up centres and limiting collateral damage.

.... .. -... . / .. -. / .--. .-... .- .. -. / ... .. --. .... −

The code of the transmitter sequences was passed from the contact office in Washington direct to Fort Meade in Maryland to the ECHELON headquarters which had technology for tracking and satellite intercepts.

Here, the simple code for the two consignments passed for verification to a duty desk and then authorised such that a transmitter could be started in each consignment.

This would give a third party with the right permissions access to the consignment location and could allow a special group to be dispatched to locate the items.

The first surprise was that the two beacons were co-located, not as expected in Riyadh, but that they had moved to the White Desert just outside Cairo. Using advanced telemetry, a satellite-based sweep of the desert was planned on a high-resolution setting. Because of satellite positioning, it took three hours before the right satellites were in a good position to run surveillance.

"Live and hot!", shouted the duty sergeant who had loaded the code and co-ordinates as the first images came in. The desert showed some small buildings, but also a clear image of a single truck, parked.

General Simpson was heading the American part of the operation. "Who do we have in the area?", he asked. "Overt or covert?" came the reply.

"This is very covert," said Simpson, "We need to blow up a couple of US manufactured consignments which were stored in Saudi Arabia and are now illegally in Egypt. The consignments are a high technology design which could be part of a terrorist plot. We need to act with maximum focus to neutralise this."

"We have some operatives in the area fit for this purpose ," came the reply, "I'm looking through the files and in country we have a small base, and some regular soldiers who could be asked to work 'native'," suggested O'Malley.

"No, I want a top person for this, we must fly someone in-black-op style. Normal airlines, under cover, provisioned with non-American weaponry in country."

The trail was now leading towards a delta force person and before very long the name Chuck Manners had surfaced. He had many awards for bravery in the field.

He was tracked down to an American military base in Germany area and called in for a briefing.

"You'll be at Stuttgart, Echterdingen airport tonight on the first plane to Cairo. You'll be provisioned with civilian transport and undesignated non-American armaments to get to a spot in the desert where you will be asked to destroy two consignments."

Chuck paused and then nodded. "This is an illegal operation?" he queried.

"Yes, it is, but there are very high stakes involved."

"If I do this and get captured, what happens?"

"You won't. You have perfect co-ordinates for the consignments and will have enough personal fire - power if anyone pays you a visit. No-one even knows the consignments have been stolen, let alone their new whereabouts. We have just diverted satellites to get this information. The consignments are currently parked, but we expect them to be moved again later today.

Chuck Manners nodded. He was used to these types of operations. He had no qualms about driving a hard position to get things done. He would work alone. He could be very fast and nimble. When involved in this type of operation, the trick was to get in and get out fast before anyone noticed.

One hour later Manners was at the airport for the flight to Cairo

Ed Adams

Park Lane

Park Lane is the second most valuable property in the London edition of the board game Monopoly.

The street still has a prestigious social status similar to when the British version of the Monopoly board was first produced, in 1936.

On the board, Park Lane forms a pair with Mayfair, the most expensive property in the game.

From Wikipedia, the free encyclopaedia

Car chase victims

Muhammad Mubarain knew the points where he could gather information and made personal calls. Despite the reputation of terrorist cells being very secure, there were many ways that gossip travelled and the people he would speak to would know if there was anything unusual.

Muhammad made his first call with Firas Belhassen, a leading Imam in the local community. He changed the story enough to avoid direct traceability, but with enough of a ring of truth to attract corrections and further confirmation.

Firas Belhassen listened and after a long pause said, "You know, I think something is happening. A few days ago we heard that Ghali Yassim would visit the UK and sure enough he arrived with his brother and a close associate named Mehdi Akren.

The Square

"Initially, they seemed to spend their time doing tourist things, spending money, gambling and behaving in a fairly non-Muslim way.

"Besides their time in Central London, they seem to have been out for several long drives to other parts of the country and instead of flying out of the UK, they have left by car into Europe. This is unusual transport for Ghali Yassim, for whom speed is the essence.

Muhammad understood the significance of this information. A senior, royal and diplomatically secure person had arrived in the UK, with supporters. He was suspected of terrorist involvement, yet had moved around freely, finally leaving the country, by car, through to France.

"Do we know when Yassim left?", Muhammad asked.

"I'm not sure, but it was in the last few days", replied Firas Belhassen. Muhammad knew that Firas wanted to lead a straightforward life, to be involved with the local community and that he deplored efforts of extremists to undermine the community and relationships within the country.

Muhammad knew it was still a tough decision for Firas to make these disclosures, because Yassim was a fellow Muslim, whereas Muhammad would provide the information to non-Muslim authorities in the United Kingdom.

Muhammad knew that he needed to get the information relayed back to Karen and the primary investigation team. They now had three names and a location and probable cargo. It was possible that the cargo had left the country with the three suspects and that it was travelling by car to France.

While Muhammad was investigating, Karen was busy too. She received notification of another incident involving Arabs in Central London. There had been a car chase involving a Mercedes and a BMW through the centre of London. Along Park Lane, the Mercedes has run into a set of railings and the people in the BMW had stopped behind the car, calmly got out, walked to the Mercedes appearing to be carrying handguns.

The commotion of the chase had created a general alert in the area and several Police motorcycles on embassy and royal duties had been able to reach the scene more or less as the car crash occurred. They had also radioed to an armed response unit which was also on its way from around a less than a mile away. The incident was close to many embassies and there was plenty of police cover.

The pursuing occupants of the BMW had seen that they were about to be out manoeuvred and had driven into a nearby underground car park. They had abandoned their car and then used a pedestrian exit to leave the car park, before anyone realized what was happening. Then they boarded a taxi from an adjacent hotel and moved quietly out of the area.

The Square

The police had created a cordon around the crashed car and had also radioed for a paramedic. The three Arabs in the car had been heavily shaken by the crash but were fundamentally uninjured compared with the heavy damage sustained by the car.

Karen had been among the first on the scene and her initial instincts were to be suspicious of what was happening. She approached the Arabs, who were trying to make excuses and to leave the scene.

"No", she instructed the Police, "We need to question these about another matter". She radioed for SI6 backup and another Paramedic ambulance arrived, driven by her own staff.

The Arabs were instructed to get into the ambulance and then it moved away followed by Karen. They would take them to a hospital ward, with the small difference that it would be within an SI6 complex. The wards were fully camera and sound enabled, which would mean if there was anything to learn from the Arabs, then they would hear it.

The ambulance cut through London traffic; Karen followed in her car. She did not understand what had been happening, why they were being chased or who the assailants were.

The hospital looked very realistic. Karen watched the three Arabs being escorted in and then being moved to individual rooms, close together. The cameras and sound were already running and within minutes they had started to talk to one another about what they needed to do. They spoke Arabic to one another, but the SI6 facility had already provided translators.

"This is not good", said one of the three. He was wearing a suit and looked very smart. "I agree", said the second, "I think they were Mossad. We need to get out of here fast."

The third Arab spoke. "We still have the rendezvous in Ashford, tomorrow".

The first Arab spoke again. "We must just leave here. Because of the car chase, we will be detained for questions, but because we are the victims, we should be able to negotiate our way out fast. My preference is to tell them we are shaken up and that we would rather answer questions tomorrow. That gives us a chance to completely leave the country."

Karen was pleased with how this was going. Without so much as a word of interrogation, they were telling her a lot about their plans. Karen's team had been running checks on the Mercedes too, and discovered that it was a recently purchased new vehicle, from a Central London garage. It included all the extras, and this included a built-in phone, which was still in the car when the police were getting ready to tow it away. Karen had requested an immediate phone trace, both of calls and of their originating location. This had shown that there was a long string of calls to many numbers, both in London but also to the middle east. In among the series were several calls from the M2 and A2, leading out of East London, through Kent and towards Dover. There were also a series of calls from a location near to Ashford.

"We have a fix on a location, and we know there will be a meeting tomorrow", thought Karen, "Now we need to know what they are expecting". She decided it was time to speak directly to the Arabs. She had already radioed to Muhammad, who was also on his way to the special facility.

Karen decided that they may get more information by using Muhammad, particularly if he could befriend them in some way. To stall until his arrival, she had a doctor visit them, say that they each needed an x-ray and that after this they would be free to go, but until this had been completed, he could not release them because of liability.

The Arabs talked amongst themselves. Then the one in the suit shrugged, "Please try to hurry, we have other appointments this evening". The Arabs had decided it would be easier to leave after the procedure had finished and with no fuss and not raising any further suspicions. At this time Muhammad arrived. Karen explained what was happening and that Muhammad could probably intervene in a way that would get further information. They decided to send him in as a medic, and he donned some hospital clothing to look the part.

He walked into the holding area where the three men were kept.

"Hello", he said, then overtly noticing they were Arabs he added *"as-salām 'alaykum"*.

The three Arabs all turned together as they heard this.

"wa 'alaykum as-salām", one of them replied. "It looks as if you could be here overnight", continued Muhammad, in English.

"They have just told me they want to do some further tests before they will let you go, in case of concussion. You won't be able to leave without the paperwork."

He continued. He was trying to create more of a feeling of being trapped and the Arabs seemed to respond to this.

"What do you mean?" asked one.

"You are to be fully examined before you can move, in case there is concussion or internal bleeding from the accident. The Arabs again consulted one another, this time in English. Then the one with the suit said, "Perhaps you can help us?"

"Sure " said Mohammed, switching back to Arabic, "what do you need?".

The Square

"We have to be at a meeting tomorrow afternoon by 16:00 and need to leave here tonight to prepare for it", said the suited Arab, "Can you help us get processed this evening?"

"I should be able to," continued Muhammad, "I am duty medic this evening, can you give me a little more information so I can complete a form to get you processed?"

He smiled to the three of them and continued to speak in Arabic. "What is the nature of your visit to UK?", he asked.

The Arabs again looked towards one another, "Business - We need to attend a meeting tomorrow afternoon, where we are to receive some goods".

"Business - that's all I need", said Muhammad, looking officious and studiously writing something onto his note pad. "I will go away now to get the paperwork produced so that you can be processed quickly".

Before he turned, he said *"ma'a as-salāmah"*, and the three Arabs replied with the same greeting.

Muhammad walked slowly to the door and then into the corridor. He had enough to go on. The three Arabs were expecting to pick up something at 16:00 tomorrow from somewhere in Ashford and they had located the pickup point from the car's mobile phone.

Muhammad relayed the information to Karen Martin. "This is great," replied Karen, "Now we have what we need to be at the pickup in Kent tomorrow".

So that is how Muhammad found himself on the Honda approaching the truck lay-by.

Mossad

The Arabs knew exactly who had been chasing them in central London.

Ghali Yassim was speaking, "They were the Israeli Intelligence Services and the reason we were being chased was because someone has made the connection between the missing nerve agent and Al Aktar. I guess the original theft has been planned for so long that someone has let it slip."

"But why would Israel be so interested?" asked Mehdi Akran.

Ghali Yassim responded, "Israel has long been on the cutting edge of research and development in advanced technologies. It may be a country of very limited natural and financial resources, and not at peace with some of its neighbours. However, Israel's scientists and engineers have faced the challenge of devising new and innovative solutions, which has led to research for military technologies, both for defence and as part of offensive border enforcement."

"Inevitably, having fought three major wars in the first two decades of its existence, the Israeli government reached the conclusion in the late 1960s that it would have to develop as much of its own defence capabilities as possible and it is through that time that we can see the closer affiliations with the USA.

"It was this combination of biotechnology research and prior warfare related research that had led to the establishment of special facilities such as the Ron Hebron Research Park where the advanced research had taken place and finally led to an accident.

"A nerve agent had been tested but then leaked with disastrous consequences. A complete lab was sealed and the remaining nerve agent packaged, ready for destruction. The tough deal for Israel was that the nerve agent would be destroyed by another country, ironically because their own capability had been sealed off because of the accident.

"The nerve agent produced had surpassed the Israeli's own expectation of strength and virulence. To destroy it required a highly specialised capability, of which there were only a few in the world. The UK's Porton Down had been selected after pressure from the United States. Although the USA could also handle the chemical agent, it had been agreed that a low-key process through the UK would attract less attention.

"We know that Avi Abner had negotiated the transfer of the canisters to the UK, via diplomatic channels
"Careless Americans," said Mehdi Akran, "Creating a deadly toxin, then leaving it in Saudi Arabia, before dumping a deadly quantity in Tel Aviv. Then leaving diplomatic channels to clear up the mess."

Ghali Yassim spoke, "It makes Al Aktar's decision simple. Steal it from Israel. That's why we ship it through various countries like regular freight. It also insulates the theft and transaction from Al Aktar."

Ghali Yassim continued, "Avi Abner's counter-intelligence services are good. Very good. But they have gambled on finding the links back to Al Aktar. Now they have tracked Al Aktar representatives to London, but they have given away their cover by the car chase involving the Mercedes and BMW. I suspect Avi Abner had wanted to act unilaterally to gather intelligence and took our arrival in London as a sign that the containers had arrived."

Ed Adams

New York bed

After the horrific incidents in Egypt, James had a simple plan to create distance and to monitor his sources for any reports of what had happened.

The helicopter strike on the truck in the desert and the cold-blooded gunning down of Karen Martin would make normal news feeds unless the authorities were trying to pull a security curtain over what had happened.

James had left Cairo rapidly and knew that by the time he reached New York he could easily be ahead of the news, even in an internet world, particularly because of the lower interest in 'foreign' news in the USA, unless Americans were directly involved.

James had a simple plan when he arrived in New York. He would go to Léa's. He and Léa had been close for two years, but when Léa moved away from London to New York, they had both agreed to part as friends.

The Square

It wasn't one of those said but not meant things. James and Léa had always been clear about their relationship and their different worlds but had seen the time together as a sensible collision and a lot of fun.

Léa was a designer for an advertising agency and a smart highflyer. James had a role seemingly as a management consultant, but he found it difficult to manage the dual-role deception with Léa , especially when they lived together in the same apartment.

Léa also has a busy and itinerant lifestyle. The work and her contracts took her to several major centres, principally New York, Frankfurt and a fair amount of work in London too. Léa also enjoyed skiing and water-sports, so there were parts of the year when she would head to Klosters or the Mediterranean for extended breaks.

Neither James nor Léa had any shortage of money and could easily move around a wide circle of friends and a broad range of locations. James preferred that Léa did not meet too many of his ex-military or special forces friends because that would give the game away. James soon found out that although Léa was very sporting, she detested soccer and that had given him a cliched alibi to meet some of his more specialised acquaintances. It was similar with Léa and her yoga and meditation, which James could appreciate but which was an area of Léa's life that he stayed away from.

They had been together for around two years until the end of last year. There had been a great opportunity for Léa in Manhattan and she had really wanted to make the move. It was great money in a vibrant city. James had initially accompanied her, but they had both known that this was probably the beginning of the end of their full-time relationship.

They had both been very good about it. Neither of them had anyone else in mind when they said final farewells and Léa had said to James that, anywhere, she would be there for him.

She had given him a key to her apartment in lower Manhattan. It was really a gesture, but at the time it made James feel good.

James took a taxi from JFK and asked for the address in SoHo where Léa lived. He had another mobile phone with him and had called the number but only picked up the answer phone. He thought it would be good to see Léa but wondered what he would find when he approached her building.

The taxi driver knew the way to the general area but was slightly confused with the street names in this unstructured part of Manhattan. James directed the last couple of turns, which had caused the driver making the equivalent of an extended U turn around a block because he had missed the turn the first time around. James paid the driver and stepped onto the sidewalk.

He looked at the building, and a strange sense of emotion washed over him. Léa had represented comfort for him when he was involved in some other tough situations and now he was standing outside her apartment some three and a half thousand miles from where he lived and he was about to say hello again for the first time, when he was in some kind of trouble.

He climbed the steps to the entrance to the apartment building and wondered whether to let himself in or whether to ring the bell. He knew the bell was the right answer and tried it twice, with no response. "OK", he thought, "I shall check things out."

He opened the main door and took the elevator to Léa's floor. The hallway was immaculate in this well-heeled and gentrified block. He approached the door and opened the lock. There was an alarm too, and he disabled this with Léa's birthday date, American-formatted, a little joke they had had when back in London.

The whole apartment looked very similar to the last time he had visited. He called out loudly in case anyone else was around, but Léa was out and that she was living there alone. He snuck a look in the wardrobes and the coat closet, but apart from a pair of his old boots, useful in snow, there was nothing else to show anyone other than Léa was living in the apartment.

Next, he checked if Léa's laptop Apple mac was around; this was a good sign that Léa was working; she always carried the machine if she was on business. A desk and a charger looked forlorn, and he knew that Léa was out somewhere on business. That could be local, but could equally be anywhere.

He flipped the telephone answering machine. Just one message from a Fed-Ex delivery, but nothing else. In the old days that could have meant she was only out for a short time, but now, with voicemail, it was less of an indication. James decided he would leave a prominent message and then return later in the evening.

If Léa was around, she would pick up the message and be able to call him. He knew she would not hesitate for a second to contact him but if she was prepared to tolerate his proximity for a few days, it could help the overall situation whilst he needed to stay under cover and not traceable.

James had used a false passport when he arrived in New York. He had dual nationality, with a right to a Canadian and a British passport and with a small amount of adaptation, his Canadian passport which had him as "Jamie" also gave a reasonable level of subterfuge to his whereabouts. He hoped that his traceability from Egypt was low and that no-one would expect him to travel to the United States.

The Square

There was, however, a drawback to his plan. The passport he was using from Canada had an embedded chip. As soon as he had handed it to the custom and immigration person in JFK, it had been activated on the passport scanner and had sent a digital stream into the main NSA tracking systems. This linked him with his slightly changed name, with Egypt, and the route he had taken was immediately detected.

Two homeland security guards had noticed when the passport had been scanned. There had been some strange developments in Egypt over the last few days, and some key individuals were being singled out for further investigation. His own Canadian passport had been the basis to trip the tracking of him and the two men were right now positioned one at the entrance to the apartment block and the second on the very floor where Léa's apartment was located.

James decided he would take a more detailed look around Léa's apartment. He was actually somewhat fuzzy from the flight and thought he would make himself some coffee to shake away the cobwebs. He knew that Léa would be fine about him making himself at home, but he also didn't want to surprise her with his entrance to her apartment.

"All in its time", he thought as he filled the coffee machine with fresh ground coffee and water and then looked in the refrigerator for some milk. None there, in fact the refrigerator was empty. Interesting, it looked as if Léa was away. He looked around for other evidence while the coffee brewed. He considered this to be good fortune if he wanted to lie low for a few days. With Léa away, he could use her apartment, and this would almost guarantee he was off of the grid and undetectable.

James had not allowed for the passport and his detection. He watched as the coffee finished filling the glass flask and then selected a mug with "I love NY" and poured in the coffee. He normally drank coffee with a dash of milk, but this would do until he could visit a nearby store. He sipped the liquid and felt an almost immediate jolt from the caffeine. Like himself, Léa liked robust coffee, and this Java was doing the trick.

He walked around for a few more minutes while looking at the rest of the apartment. Very tidy, lived in, but neat. He went out to a nearby store. He could buy provisions and also some flowers as a peace offering for Léa, based upon his breaking and entering her apartment.

James took the elevator back to ground level and was emerging back to the street, when a man in front of him called out, "Hey Bud, do you know where 3rd Street is?" He looked up, tensing in case this was a trap. He knew he was operating below his normal reflexes and realised about half a second before the move that a second man was standing just behind him. The two men neatly scooped James into a nearby car and locked the doors.

"Mr Goodwin," started the first man, "Welcome to New York, there are a few people we would like you to meet."

The Square

"Who are you?" questioned James, "And what do you want?"

"Relax," said the first man, "You will come to no harm and all we require is some limited information."

The car, a large square looking Ford, a Crown Victoria, waddled along the bumpy streets of Manhattan, James couldn't get used to the sea-sick feeling of American suspension, even in this challenging situation.

"Look, I don't know who you are or what you want, but I'm in Manhattan to see a friend," he continued.

"We know you were in Cairo," said one of the Americans, "We know you were in the desert and that the truck pick up went wrong. We have photos of the damage, both the truck and the Israeli helicopter," he continued.

James didn't know that the helicopter was Israeli and had no idea who had fired the missile that blasted the helicopter from the sky.

"Who are you?", asked James. He didn't feel in direct danger, because if the men had intended something terrible, they would have started on him by now.

They looked American, had American accents, east coast. He could see them, there was no bag over his head and they had not stabbed him with a hypodermic syringe or anything worse. There were no visible guns, although he suspected that his abductors would have easy access to firepower.

He would give them something, but not much. He knew there was no point in denying this, and that all he was doing was prolonging the inevitable.

"So, if I was in Cairo, what links me to whatever you are talking about?"

"Let's just say we had a very experienced operative in the area, and he followed you back to Cairo. He was also nearby when the woman was shot by a high-powered rifle. We are trying to join some pieces together and we need to know what you were expecting in the pickup. Your transport was a regular car, so I don't think you were expecting the actual cargo of the truck."

It mystified James. He knew that the desert exchange that had gone wrong was supposed to be a swap of some holdall or case, but he had not been told its contents.

"I was expecting a small delivery," he replied, "Something I could carry, but I have no idea what the consignment comprised. I expected it to be papers or film or maybe DVDs or similar."

"So, the rather larger contents of the truck were not of interest?" continued the first American.

The Square

"I don't think I know what you mean", replied James, thinking there was something that he had not been told. "What was in the truck?"

"The truck contained a missile", replied the second American, speaking for the first time since they had been together in the car.

"A serious piece of weaponry, so serious that it had built in trackers which were activated when it started to move around. It was from the Saudi Arabian Air Force."

"So, what was it doing in Egypt, in a truck?", asked James, genuinely confused and thinking these Americans couldn't know much about what was happening. Unreliable witnesses, he decided.

"We thought you might tell us," said the second American. "Look we know all about you, that you freelance, have been in a few scrapes but don't really do violent things."

"Just dangerous things." added the first American.

"Look, I'm co-operating," said James, "Just who are you?"

"We're from the NSA - the National Security Agency," explained the first American. "We are local agents sent out to talk to you. I don't think you know how serious this is."

"I'm getting the picture," said James, "If you've been that speedy following me, then there has to be something big occurring. Show me some identity, please."

The first American showed a metal badge and an identity card. It all looked genuine, but James realized he wouldn't really know if the papers he was being shown were real. But the identity card had a hologram and looked fairly high-technology.

"I'll co-operate," said James, "I'll tell you what I know." The car pulled over at a small cafe on the edge of Central Park. The two Americans stepped out and beckoned to James. "Let's have coffee," said the first American, "No funny business, though," added the second.

"We're cool," said James as they sat down at a small table. "Three Americanos," said the second American to the waiter.

"Okay, so I'm Scott and he's Nick," the first American started to explain, "So James, tell us what you know,"

James was certain now that these two were low-level operatives. They didn't seem to know much about the situation and were cross-examining him in a coffee-shop.

James started to describe the situation he'd been in. He changed as little as possible, in case he was asked the same things again, which was a frequent interrogation technique. He decided that he would be prepared to disclose everything except Karen's name and the amount they paid him. But he needed to say another sum, which seemed low enough to make him seem small-time. He settled on £10,000.

"So, I was already known to the UK authorities. I do some driving for them when they want to be anonymous. I'm reliable. On this occasion I was instructed by a woman. I don't know here name, not her real one anyway. Just that she was called Mrs Clinton. I knew that was a code name.

"The drop was to take place in the desert. I was given GPS co-ordinates and a time. I took a car and waited. Then I saw the truck and then the helicopter. The chopper fired on the truck. Just one missile. Then a surface-to-air from about a mile away took out the helicopter.

"The helicopter had locked on my car before it was destroyed. I think I would have been next. I drove away fast after the helicopter fell, before the guy with the SAM could get creative."

"So what was the pickup?" asked Nick.

"It was supposed to be small, a holdall or a case. That was all. It was something I could carry. I didn't ever see it."

The two Americans looked at one another. "So you were not expecting the truck to contain a missile?"

"Absolutely not," said James, "And my instructions were to swap the goods, not to take over the truck."

Scott said to Nick, "This seems plausible. The consignment was small, and that is consistent with what we've been told from the site in Egypt. You can go back to the apartment. Stay in the vicinity for the next few days, we will make some further investigations, but your story is consistent from one we have from another source."

The other source was another freelancer, ex American military named Chuck Manners. Since he'd been sent to Cairo, he had also been told that the consignment was small and that it was easy to locate via a tracker beacon. That is how he had been tracking it until the appearance of the helicopter. He was certain that the unit destroyed was the source of the beacon. Now Scott, Nick, Chuck and James were all reaching the same conclusion. That they had been following the wrong GPS beacon.

"Okay," said James, "I'll go back to the apartment. I'll stay a few days, but I'm expecting you to be watching. And looking out for me."

James was back at Léa's apartment. As he opened the door, he noticed that there were some differences. Where he had picked up the pile of travel documents and moved them to the desk, they were now back on the table. He called out for Léa. Maybe she had returned during his rather unexpected absence. There was no reply, and he wondered how the papers could have moved, or whether he had somehow imagined it.

The Square

He flicked through the stack and noticed some documentation related to a trip by Léa to Cannes, France. She was away right now and not expected back for several days. He thought about calling her, but decided, given the other circumstances, that it would be better to stay as dark as possible. Léa's absence gave him a chance to lie low with the minimum of people knowing his whereabouts.

Downstairs, the two members of Mossad were already relaying the information about Léa to their contact in Nice, France. Mossad, the Israeli secret service had also followed James to the apartment. It had been easy, they'd tracked James' departure from Cairo to New York, spotted the two men that were following James, placed a small radio beacon on both of them in the airport and then followed them across Manhattan to Léa's apartment.

Once James had entered it, they waited for him to go out, in order to do some breaking and entering and to find the papers about Léa. They would use this to gain some leverage over James.

Unwind

James decided to lay low in Léa's apartment. He still could not contact her because of the threat of being followed or traced. He could see the date she was due to return from her vacation and he was looking forward to seeing her. He was not contacted again by the Americans and had been treating his time as a kind of vacation in New York.

The last few days had been both tiring and shocking and time to unwind seemed like the perfect antidote. He suspected that he was being observed, but didn't let that deter him from moving around Manhattan. He did nothing related to the events in Cairo. He had checked the news including the Cable feed from Al Jazeera, but there was no mention of the truck or helicopter incident.

James still had the case from the desert. It was the one he was supposed to exchange with the truck driver.

Now, he decided, was the time to open it. To find out what the fuss was about. He would need assistance for this. The case might be rigged. He would need to contact Karen's handler back in the UK. To arrange a meeting and a hand-over.

James checked the phone that Karen had given him. It included a second number. SERVICE DESK. He knew what it meant. The standard protocol for expedited calls to Karen's Handler.

He dialled it.

"Karen's florists. Jane speaking, how may I direct your call?"

"I need to speak to the owner."

" What Karen? - I'm afraid she is out."

"No, Karen's boss. Karen says we need more petals."

"One moment please, please hold."

There was silence on the line. A click.

"Hello, who is that speaking?"

"I'm an associate of Karen Martin. I was in the desert. My name is James,"

"Hello James, I am sorry for your loss."

"I have something of interest to the company. I would like to bring it along and get it opened, Karen gave it to me."

"Ah yes, we know about that item, can you describe it for me?"

"Yes, it is a case. A briefcase."

"Yes, it is tamper-proof. Can you look at the front lock? There should be a small number stamped underneath the catch, next to a USB port."

"Yes, there is, TRQ73845. And a small USB port next to it."

"That's the right number. We would like to arrange collection."

"Okay, please let me give the collectors something for identification."

"Of course, what would you like?"

"A lampshade," said James, looking for inspiration around the room.

"I will make sure that the collector can tell you that."

"Now, we need an address for a pickup."

The Square

"Tomorrow evening - 19:00 Molly's - 3rd and East 22nd - I'll have the case in a Macy's white star tote."

"That's very clear. Someone will see you tomorrow evening."

Chuck goes to MI6

Robert Alton was informed of the arrangements made with James. He was considering whether to send someone from the embassy for the pickup. He'd requested a USB stick coded with the unlock logic for the case, which he had collected in person from the technical department.

As Robert Alton re-entered SI6, there was a message waiting for him at the front reception.

"You have a visitor Mr.Alton; a Mr. Manners. He is sitting over there. He says the appointment was made at the last minute."

Alton looked towards Chuck Manners. He didn't recognise him. Suntanned in a suit, he looked like a military man.

"Er, Mr Manners. I don't think we have a meeting booked. Perhaps there is some mistake?" asked Alton. He looked towards Manners, who stood and walked towards him.

"Good morning, Mr Alton, I think you'll want to talk to me," said Manners. "I'm just back from the desert. I think you know where. It would be useful to talk."

"In my office?" asked Alton, "Or maybe it's better to go outside?"

"I'd prefer outside too," said Manners.

Manners removed his visitor pass, handed it to the reception and walked through the revolving doors to leave the building.

"You're not from the Agency?" said Alton.

"Correct. I've just come back from Cairo. Look, I was involved in the op. Don't pretend you don't know. Karen was there. You Brits were set up."

Alton looked at Manners carefully. "Who are you? The stringer? You worked for Karen?"

"No," said Manners, "I didn't find out about Karen, or her stringer buddy James until after the mission. I thought I was working alone, and that it was for the Americans."

"Why would you be telling me this, now?" asked Alton, "If you are working for the Americans, then I'd expect them to pass the information through normal channels."

"Ordinarily, so would I. Except there are no normal channels for this. There's something wrong. The people who paid me to go to Egypt have disappeared. My field contact in Cairo has disappeared. The only person I've found was one of your people, still in Cairo. I told him to get out."

Alton looked again at Manners. "What were you doing in Cairo? Were you part of what happened to Karen?"

"Not at all. I was there to prevent the truck in the desert from being destroyed. I was under orders from DoD to bring down the helicopter. I was told that the truck contained something of National Security to the United States."

"So, the Americans sent you to bring down the helicopter? Why would they do that? It would certainly antagonise a lot of people."

"Not as many as you might think. I was told that the truck contained something important to America. Something whose delivery was being intercepted by a hostile force. To be honest, I'd no idea that the Brits were also involved in this.

"I know it wasn't one of your helicopters - even in the stealth paint. An Apache, but it was one of the Longbows, really jazzed engines, swept rotor tips and the extra radar bubble for target acquisition. Top specification. It was playing for a fast kill and exit. We Americans have them, but I don't know if anyone else has these high spec versions."

Manners continued, "To be honest, what started out as a clean mission has become very dirty. The truck was destroyed by a very purposeful hunter platform, and then the Brits were chased back to Cairo. Originally, I didn't think anyone wanted this to leak out. I've changed my mind now, though. That's why I've brought this to SI6. There's something deeply wrong with the American intel around this."

Alton looked at Manners, " You need to tell me, but first, how did you link this to SI6 and trace it back to me here?"

"Cairo is a small city if you are involved with our kind of work. It didn't take me long to follow the link to Karen's local help. Think about it. I also needed local support. SAMs are not that easy to walk through as hand luggage.

"My local guy put two and two together and worked out who would have been helping the woman that was shot. Curiously enough, he thought the sniper was another woman - a mercenary named Katarina Voronin.

"I followed the trail and although one of your guys had skipped the country, the other was still lying low. Waiting for payment. 'Follow the money' still works.

"It was lucky for me, because if he had skipped then there would be no links left. After I met him, I told him to lose himself, or he'd be next on the hit list.

"He told me about your mission to collect something from the truck. That there was supposed to be a hook-up in the desert. I don't believe it would have happened, even without the helicopter being present. I think the Brits were there to witness what happened - no more and no less."

Alton interrupted, "Why would that be? What is the point of setting up such an elaborate scheme?"

"I think this was a demonstration. Ahead of something else. There's going to be some kind of downstream threat. Or maybe there has already?"

Alton shook his head, "Frankly, if this was true, then you'd know far more about what is happening than we do. I agree it looks as if they set us up. The fact you have shown up here is pretty rich considering the trouble you are in."

Manners responded, "Sure - and that's why you need me on the outside. I'm more use to you in the field than locked away in some suite in SI6. My self-interest is running this down so I get out in one piece. Whoever ended Karen probably has a long list that includes me - and your other Cairo buddies."

Manners continued, "Believe me, I wouldn't have brought this to you unless I thought something terrible is going down. You guys seem set up as the 'validators'. People who have witnessed what might happen. My guess is the hostile playbook will say, 'contact you, show they know all about Cairo and then start making new demands against a bigger threat.'"

Alton nodded, "You could be right. I'll be honest with you. You have already filled in some gaps. I have one other piece you haven't picked up. The helicopter. It wasn't American, it was Israeli."

Manners pretended to look startled. He had already seen the black overpainted markings on the crashed 'copter. He decided it was better to play along, "An Israeli helicopter on a stealth assault in Egyptian airspace. You have got to be kidding me."

"My reaction too. They dressed it to look like mercenaries and will deny everything, but this was one well-funded and high-tech mission."

"Okay," said Manners, "I'm staying involved in this for two reasons. One: America seems to be handling this as a black op. Two: It's turning into a threat against me too.

"That's why I've come to you. I've already given you a lot of information. I'll ask you to provide me some cover as this plays out. I may need to disappear by the end of this."

Alton looked at Manners, "I respect you coming to see me like this, Mr Manners."

"Ordinarily I could not agree to work with you, though. Understand my position on this. A blown operation, casualties, new threats and then an unknown American turns up out of the blue offering assistance. Furthermore, he knows more than the intelligence agencies about what happened in Cairo 48 hours ago."

"Now here is the thing. I have Karen's stringer making contact with us. His name is James, and he is British. He still has the briefcase, which he was supposed to exchange with the truck driver in the desert. It's a booby-trapped device which will destroy its contents if opened without a special electronic key.

The case contains a series of decommission codes for the canisters in transit. I am arranging for our embassy in New York to pick them up. We will then have the codes, which I think can disable the canisters.

"These are the canisters in transit across the desert from Saudi Arabia?" asked Chuck.

"That's right," answered Alton.

"Well, the explosion of the first canister was a regular fireball," answered Chuck.

"It looked as if they were trying to incinerate something."

"What was it?" asked Chuck, "A further weapon of some kind - I don't think it was a missile, despite what has been put out there?"

The Square

"Yes," answered Alton, "We think the truck was carrying a binary neurotoxin. The case also contains the codes to disable the neurotoxin."

"You said it is a binary. Does that mean there are codes to enable it as well?" asked Chuck, "I've worked at Los Alamos and know about some of these chemical weapons, from a distance."

"You are right," answered Alton. "There's one set of codes to arm the toxin and a different set to destroy it. The codes are all in that case which James holds.

"So, some bad people want the case now?" asked Chuck.

"That's what we think, the toxin was on its way to being destroyed but now it has been intercepted."

"But if it has been destroyed, then surely the codes are worthless?" asked Chuck.

"Normally I'd agree, but there is a second truck with a further 10 canisters of neurotoxin."

"… And where is that?" asked Chuck.

"We've no idea, " answered Alton, "The trace on the second truck has gone cold."

"I think James might need some help," said Chuck, "Can I visit him?"

"I thought you were working for the US on this?" asked Alton.

"I was, but things just got more complex," answered Chuck, "Where is James now?"

"New York," answered Alton, "We've arranged to pick up the case from a meeting with him, in a bar."

"Next flight tonight, then," answered Chuck,"BA around 1900 if I remember correctly, from T5 - I can just make it. You'd better get me the unlock code for the briefcase and tell me the rendezvous."

"Use this," said Alton handing over the small USB stick he had collected earlier that morning,

"Just plug it in and then the case should open. That flight should get you in by midnight. You'll have most of tomorrow to locate James and meet him at the bar, Molly's bar," Alton handed Manners the address and contact details to meet James.

Manhattan

"Steel, glass, tile, concrete
will be the materials of the
skyscraper.
Crammed on the narrow island the
millionwindowed buildings
will be just glittering,

pyramid on pyramid

like the white cloudhead
above a thunderstorm"

— John Dos Passos, Manhattan Transfer

Molly's

Evening in New York. James was in the Irish bar. He'd already bought a glass of black beer and was sipping it, waiting for someone to arrive. Prominently on the chair next to him was a Macy's tote. Bright red, with a white star on it, and inside it a metal briefcase.

"Good evening," said a voice. James looked towards a tall figure, slightly tanned and with a clipped American accent.

"Do you mind if I sit here? I've been shopping for lighting. Someone asked me to get a lampshade,"

"And you are?" asked James.

"I'm Chuck Manners," came the reply, "I think we met once before briefly. In the desert. I was pre-occupied, and I think you drove away."

"Mr Manners," answered James, "I assume we both know some of the same people,"

"It's Colonel, but you can call me Chuck," smiled Chuck back towards James.

"It has been an intense couple of days, for both of us I'm sure."

Chuck replied, "They have asked me to retrieve the case; I think I might assist defuse it too."

"Okay, but I think you should know that there is someone following me. They have come across to New York from Egypt. They were in my girlfriend's apartment."

"Okay, we will need to resolve that," answered Chuck, "Do you know who they were or what they want?"

"Not exactly, although they seem to be after some codes."

"I think I know what that is about," answered Chuck, They are codes to disable the content of the truck that was blown up by the helicopter."

"So, they must know that, why do they still want the codes?" asked James.

"There were two; two trucks and two consignments. I think they have lost the other consignment at the moment. If they can find it, they will want to arm it."

"That was a pretty powerful warhead," said James, "Even at three clicks it was devastating."

"I agree," said Chuck, "So we can be sure they are up to no good."

"Okay," said James, "I'll hand over the case, but I might need your help if they continue to pursue me."

"You have my word," said Chuck, looking James in the eye, " One casualty from this already, we don't want any more."

"Look, I'm staying at the W just off Times Square. Room 5111. 51st floor. I'm taking the case there now. I'll open it and then we can get back together, if you like. I'll be flying out tomorrow, back to the UK. I assume you will want to get lost, so that whoever had been tracking you can't locate you any longer. Just make sure to give me a way to stay in contact at least until we both leave New York."

James nodded and wrote something down.

"We should exchange contact details," he said.

Chuck nodded then rose, picked up the Macy's bag and raised his glass of beer, "Slàinte Mhath!" he said.

"Cheers;" said James.

The Square

Léa

Léa had first met James in London when he was sitting in a cafe drinking a latte and there was no other table spare.

She'd been in a hurry and had left a bag behind - a genuine accident.

James had called after her, and then left the cafe to pass the bag back to her. In a moment of impulse, he had invited Léa for a supper any time in the same week.

Léa had, to her slight surprise, agreed, and they had met later the same evening and over a short time developed a strong relationship.

They had made a good couple and although Léa still didn't know fully what James did as a consultant; it gave her some surprise vacation breaks as she could sometimes follow him around during his assignments.

Ed Adams

She wasn't at all phased to receive the ticketing for Cannes, from James, with its clandestine romantic message, "Not a word until we meet."

The current situation was great and after two years apart a chance to re-acquaint.

James had contacted her to offer her a visit to Cannes for a water sport break until he could join her there on his way back from Turkey. He had sent her the ticket and hotel information, and it was a great surprise.

So now Léa was enjoying every minute. Sea-spray, bumping, solid power. Cannes has been a stroke of genius.

Now she was in a smart hotel, with a private beach and enjoying as much water sports as she could handle. The complementary hotel upgrade had been a bonus on top. The powerboat lesson had been great, and she was really getting the hang of the water-skis. In the distance she could see another fast powerboat, but apart from that, she seemed to have the immediate bay to herself.

The other boat was similarly practicing water-ski manoeuvres but didn't seem to have a skier in tow. Léa assumed it was someone out to try the boat's manoeuvrability, although it was now getting closer to the area where she was practicing.

The Square

Then suddenly, it spun towards their boat and manoeuvred itself in parallel, but with a closing gap. It slowed, so that instead of being in line with her boat, it was now in line with her.

A blur of something dark. It was a net like the kind used to land a large fish. It had been fired somehow from the other boat and landed just in front of her. She was in it. The safety line to her powerboat had disconnected. She was now in the sea, in her wetsuit, floating on her buoyancy device and in a net.

She struggled to get free but could feel the net being pulled. She was being reeled in, like some captured exotic fish. The other powerboat was not visible, it was somewhere to the left of the boat that was pulling her in and she could only hear noises of engine and shouted instruction from the boat which was now her capturer.

She was hauled up the side of the boat, banging her body and then her legs and shins against the edge of the craft, then flopping with a thud to the deck surface of the boat. Without removing the net, two men had slipped a white plastic loop around her legs and her arms. She felt immense fear, what on earth was this about? She tried to scream, but nothing came out. Then darkness as she was pushed down some steps in the boat into a darkened room.

She heard the engine rev and the boat took up a quick speed away from the area, the floor of her temporary cell sloping and bumping with the progress of the boat.

Less than an hour later they stopped. The boat was being docked, and Léa guessed they were not so far from Cannes, where she had been staying, but that they had taken her to a different location for whatever purpose.

Then she heard footsteps approach and saw one of her captors descend the ships stairs towards her. "Don't worry', he said, "If you co-operate, and your friend co-operates, then no-one will get hurt. We don't want you, but you are a way to get to James and in turn to something he has which belongs to us."

Léa was mystified by this, as well as scared, "I don't know what you are talking about she said,"...and how do you know James. I think you have the wrong people. Neither of us is mixed up in anything, so I don't think holding me will get you anywhere. Just let me go!"

"I can't do that, we need to get to James, and you will help us," continued the captor. He motioned towards a video camera.

"You will make a small video now and we will use it to attract James. You must say you are in captivity, and that you want to be set free. Ask James to come here and we will arrange for your freedom. It's really that simple."

He positioned the camera on a small tripod and switched it on. "No" said Léa, "I won't ask James to help me. You must just let me go. This is illegal and you will be in a lot of trouble." Léa stared towards her captor, who kept the camera running.

"To be honest, it doesn't matter what you say," he continued, "As long as you show James you are with us. I can then add a message to the video recording."

Anonymity

After James had returned to Léa's Manhattan apartment and seen the disturbed papers, his thought was of how comprehensively he had been rumbled. His original plan to depart from Cairo and to select a pseudo-random destination had been well and truly intercepted. Not only did he have local US spooks onto him, he also believed that he was being followed by a second team or ironically that the second team had been watching the Americans who had visited him.

Either way, "Team 2" has somehow tracked him down and also broken into the apartment and found enough material to be able to track down Léa.

Even he had only just figured out that she was in France, but his main concern was that she would now be part of a trade for the information that he held about his recent aborted project.

The Square

It didn't take a genius to work out that 'Team 2' and possibly also 'Team 1' would be looking for the means to get information from James. And it would be via Léa.

He looked around the apartment. He switched on the television; he flicked on a few more lights. There. That would make the place look busy if anyone were to check his whereabouts.

He exited via the elevator but then through a back exit to the building. It brought him to a short lane which led onto another busy thoroughfare. At the end of the lane he could see yellow cabs.

He thought about the need to phone Léa. He hadn't wanted to do so from her apartment and he'd deliberately not kept a cell phone with him from the time he had started the live part of the mission.

He would head directly to the airport and phone her from the anonymity of the airport.

Take the AirTrain

James sat in the airport lounge. He'd been able to use his traveller card to gain access despite a lowly economy ticket. New York JFK was quiet for a Friday, as had been the entire drive from midtown.

The route from 42nd Street had been along to the midtown tunnel and then out across to Long Island. The long streets were lit with afternoon sun, which glinted from the skyscrapers as he looked down towards Lower Manhattan. Long Island traffic was almost at a standstill, although the cab driver wove a complicated route, dodging the worst of the clogged streets.

Instead of going directly to the terminal at JFK, he had asked the cab to drop him at the Hertz car rental depot.

He had used the AirTrain back to the terminal and the long way around to Terminal Seven via all the intermediate stops. This gave him a chance to see if he was being directly followed. No-one in their right mind would use his route so any co-incidence would probably be more than that.

It didn't take long to get around to the check-in area. Then through self-check-in, the enhanced security which involved removing shoes and into the area with the streams of water and the mini escalators rising half floor height before following the signs to the haven of the lounge.

He could tell it was a Friday in the lounge, however. There were plenty of executive types sitting around, but instead of the usual bleeps of mobile phone tunes and the murmur of business conversations, there was much more of a hush. The bluetooths had been retired for the weekend. Much of Europe was already out for a Friday evening and so the usual source of much of the conversation had already subsided.

Time's arrow was working, and the weekend was already underway in the places that many of the people in this particular lounge were travelling to. Sport pages were being read, people were reclining on beach loungers (an improbable feature of this airport lounge). It was time to power down for the next couple of days.

Sleek brown tee shirt

James knew he was still on duty. He was expecting to be contacted before he left New York. As the minutes were reducing, he wondered how this would happen. He only had the time between now and the walk to Gate Nine to board his plane. The relaxed businessman nearby was reading a book about Caesar. Maybe he was the contact?

James looked at him cautiously. He seemed engrossed in his book, and then a flight was called to Madrid and he rose and left, to be replaced almost immediately by a French mother with two children.

James noticed her commandeering the space and spreading her bags and the childrens' belongings around, then removing a chunky woollen cardigan revealing a sleek brown tee-shirt. James looked away before the woman noticed and continued to read his newspaper.

The Square

One of the children, around ten years old, was by his side and counting a few dollars conspicuously to his right. James glanced up and at the same moment met the woman's gaze.

"The bag is for you," she said, glancing towards a white carrier bag by the side of the child. It looked like a newsagent carrier bag, similar to the one he had been given when he purchased his own newspaper on the way to the lounge. The mother called something to the boy in French and he jumped up taking his younger brother by the hand walking across to the display of cookies and potato chips.

"Take the bag, now", spoke the woman softly, "and make your way to Gate Nine. The content is papers, but it includes what you are looking for," she continued softly. "Don't try to follow us - we are travelling to Paris but know nothing further of your plans. They tricked me into making this contact - I want nothing further to do with it and I'm scared that if you don't follow my instructions then something will happen to me or the boys," she added.

James nodded, swept up the carrier and then moved towards the exit from the lounge. He knew he would examine the contents when he was away from the area but realised that he was putting the woman in some danger if he didn't do what was requested.

Calling Chuck

From the airport, James called Chuck.

"Wow, that was quick," exclaimed Chuck, "Is everything all right?"

"Not really," answered James, "They've kidnapped my girlfriend, Léa, and are asking for codes, like we talked about yesterday."

"Where is she?"

"Yeah, and where am I? I'm at JFK about to leave New York for London, then Cannes, France to find her. I don't really know what I'm up against, but I might have to pick up a small toolkit on the way."

"I thought I'd best let you know, seeing as you followed me across to New York."

"Okay," said Chuck, "I'll be thinking about this and how best to deploy."

"Thanks, Chuck."

La Côte d'Azur

"Dark Sunglasses: You may want to pick up a pair of especially dark glasses (to be more discreet when appreciating the beautiful people of Aix-en-Provence)."

— Rick Steves (Provence & the French Riviera)

Croisette

James had not really slept since New York. He had fitful bursts in the economy section of the BA plane, and then while waiting in London. Now he was in Cannes. He knew he should sleep to be sharp for the next day, but a combination of adrenaline and anxiety had kept him awake. The hotel room was in a side street on the fourth floor. He had a small balcony and had wanted to keep the room unlocked to improve ventilation on what had been a warm night. But he had spooked himself and was worried about intruders. His logic was that anyone serious about finding him would not let a small hotel window deter them, but on the other hand, the glass looked thick troublesome to break and there were extra security devices on both the hotel room door and the sliding patio window.

So, after interrupted sleep, James had awoken and freshened up for the day. He could feel a dull edge in his head, which he knew was the effect of too little sleep, and he worried that this could reduce his reactions during the day's events.

At around this time, a noise from roadworks outside the hotel disturbed him and he looked down to see a series of road markers and two men drilling the road surface. He wondered if this was linked to his presence, but assumed it was coincidence. It was directly outside his hotel and meant a small village of workman's huts had been erected during the night. His vantage point meant that he could see what was involved and as well as the paraphernalia of the roadworks, there appeared to be a satellite dish and some sort of communications station.

Maybe he was paranoid now, but this did not look normal to him. He looked through the belongings he had brought with him. A small holdall and a separate, tiny rucksack. He weighed up his possessions and moved a few into the rucksack. A tee-shirt, a camera, phone, cash and credit cards and a few other small items. The rest he left in the other holdall. He looked behind him as he reversed out of the room. Goodbye room 425. He left the hotel without checking out. He was still booked for another day which gave himself longer to escape detection.

It was still only just after nine in the morning, and James decided to scope out the area designated for the meeting. His small hotel was near to the old town and the harbour. He could lose himself in this part of town until the time arrived to meet with the dangerous people who had abducted Léa. He knew why and would need to play the whole situation carefully.

The Square

Eventually he found a small area of wall, by the harbour, away from the bustle of people and with a good view towards a large clock on the hillside overlooking the old town. A perfect vantage point in the sunshine whilst he waited for the due hour to arrive. He had picked up a newspaper from a table as he left the hotel and now read this quietly.

At ten minutes to eleven, he stirred to begin his trial walk to rehearse the meeting with the abductors. He calculated it would take five or six minutes to get back to the Palais de Congress and then he could walk slowly towards the Western end of the Croisette, It would take him at least twenty minutes to walk along at a moderate speed.

A warm blue sky and just the trail of aircraft crossing Europe and the tiniest wisps of cloud. He had been told to walk the length of the Croisette promenade at 11.00 on Thursday morning and that he would be contacted. The situation seemed strangely ironic as he walked past billboards advertising the latest spy movie, along with pictures of playboys and the silhouettes of shapely women.

Cannes seemed geared for pleasure, with its combination of languid cafes, meticulously expensive shops and sunshine, even here in November. It was Wednesday, and he had time to make a survey of the area, both anxious to understand what would unfold within the next twenty-four hours but also inquisitive of the mainly relaxed lifestyle of the local inhabitants. It was clearly the end of the season. Businessmen mingled with suntanned locals, the darker tanned types who looked as if they either lived in Cannes all year and the cosmetically enriched tans of the jet setters with their expensive wrap-around sunglasses.

James was aware that he may already be under observation, but even as he pivoted and took a slightly erratic path along the promenade there was no discernible reaction from anyone except an old lady walking a very small dog which itself had been alarmed at one if his sudden movements.

James also recognized that there was a chance that he was observed from a car or even maybe a rooftop, but then, maybe the people he was dealing with were just confident enough to not consider it worth the effort .

The start of his walk had been near to the old town, where there was a harbour, many small boats moored and some small but presumably expensive seafood restaurants. He knew the area was not the primary one he had been asked to walk and in the near distance he could see the large concrete slab of the Palais de Congress, which marked the start of his route. He skirted the harbour, noticing a small and moderately camouflaged MacDonald's on his way to the start of the route. Passing the Palais, there were various business folk standing outside chatting in small groups. There was some kind of exposition in progress and these suited and sombre looking people were the overspill. Mainly smoking, they stood in small knots chatting together and across in a corner a TV crew was filming an interview with someone who James presumed to be a conference presenter.

Then he walked along the expanse of the curving Croisette. James had even noticed this from the air on his flight into Nice. The bay was a great shape for a sunny view towards the Mediterranean and the mainly low-rise hotels had a grandeur and sense of belonging. The road was wide with twin carriageways and a central median of palm trees so the whole effect was exactly what one would want for the South of France.

James continued, checking the terrain, which was flat, although at intervals with ramps from the promenade down to the beach, some 10 metres lower. Despite being November, there were bathers on the beach and several bikini clad women soaking the last rays of the year's summer-like sunshine.

As James walked, he noticed the varied transport around him. In addition to walkers, there were motor scooters, in-line skaters and cyclists. The road was often separated from the promenade by between two and twenty metres, so there was a high probability that whoever was to meet him would be on foot or aided by a bike or similar.

A couple of times James simply stopped and sat down on blue chairs which had been placed along the edge of the pavement. It gave him a chance to look around and really to see if there was anything unusual about the people around him. But his fellow walkers were of many types, with no obvious pattern. There were no para-military types or anyone looking furtive or surprised by his sudden movements. He concluded that he was not being followed and that the group would first appear the next day.

At the end of the main route, he turned, crossed the entirety of the promenade and started the walk back. He eyed the large hotels and their opulent entrances. The mainly black-clothed inhabitants of the hotels, the well-coutured women with sleek hair, tans, immaculate lip gloss and inevitable sunglasses, The clusters of sleek Mercedes and the street parked Bentley, Maserati and a row of three Ferraris. This was no ordinary town and there was clear wealth around.

He selected a café ahead. It had a slight stairway leading into it and a row of concrete garden pots along the roadside. The height gave it a slight advantage and he was able to select a small corner table which gave a great vantage of the road. His interest was two-fold. To observe the type of traffic at this time of the day and to see whether there was now any overt sign that he was being observed. Jake knew this was irrational, but alone, in an unknown place and with a situation tomorrow which could be dangerous, he felt the need to cross-examine the situation from every possible angle.

"Café au lait" he requested to the waiter, who appeared surprisingly quickly and was very attentive. James paused now with the coffee to contemplate the next 24 hours.

The Square

Then, from his cafe position, James saw a large, tanned and thickset man on roller blades moving towards him.

"Surely not?" he thought, but yes, as the man approached James, he held out an envelope and thrust it to James. James looked around. The man was already 30 metres away and still moving fast. James opened the envelope.

Inside were two items. First, a picture of Léa, in a wet suit and tied up. She looked petrified. Then a sheet of A4 paper, typed with the message, " Go down the slip to Café L'Ondine".

James looked around and realised it was one of the cafes along the beach. He had not been paying attention to their names but assumed that the one in question would be close to his current location. He looked at the next one, which was named after a hotel, as was the next one. Then one small private one and then the one he had been directed to.

From the top of the slope he could see five or six people sitting at a table and chatting, laughing, in fact. He moved down the slope and as they saw him, their demeanour became very serious, very fast.

One of them stood. "Mr Goodwin," he started, "Welcome to our dejeuner, would you care for some wine?" he offered.

James declined. "Where is Léa?" he began. "She has nothing to do with anything."

"I'm afraid she does," continued the same voice, "You implicated her by your very friendship—now we want to do a simple trade. You have something of ours, and we have something of yours. At the moment, I trust that both items are in very good condition."

"What do you need?" asked James.

"Simple, we need the code sequences for the canisters. I know your government intends to disarm them. We will want to prime them."

"And if I get them for you?" asked James.

"We'll return Léa and you can walk away. You won't be able to stop us in any case. Our interest is just in the codes and their consequences. You and Léa are just a cost of doing business."

"So how do I get the codes?" asked James.

"We thought you'd know. We both know you are well-connected. You'll either have to ask for them or steal them. And don't think about giving us the wrong information. We'll test them before we return Léa. You have until Friday - I assume you will do this by phone, not by travelling."

"Yes," said James, "That would be my method."

The Square

James thought to himself. He knew the codes would be a two-signature process, so the chances to get the information other than formally would be very unlikely to succeed.

"Okay," said James, "Give me three days. I will get the information."

"No," said the smiling voice, "You have two days - no, 1 day, 23 hours and 50 minutes. And we will end this when the clock runs out. That's *en plein midi* midday, French time, on Friday."

James nodded. He would get the codes.

He left the cafe. He wanted to check that he wasn't being followed. Then he called Chuck Manners once again.

"James?" said Chuck, "This is becoming a habit!"

"Hi Chuck, thank you for picking up, I met with Léa's captors. They have asked me for the codes. They don't know that I had them, nor that I gave them to you, but now they want them in exchange for Léa."

There was a pause, "Okay," said Chuck, "I have the codes. I could send them to you. You'd get Léa, but the captors would have access to the weapons. It also assumes they don't try to double cross. I think we need a better play than me sending the codes and you handing them over. I need to talk to Robert Alton again. "

James considered, "Okay, but I need you to promise that you'll send the codes to me by 11:50 French time Friday. It's my last chance to get Léa back."

"Here's what I'll do. It's Wednesday. I can get across to Cannes by tomorrow around midday, if I leave quickly. We can meet up and by then I'll have a plan for what to do on Friday."

Trip to London

Chuck checked the flights to get to Cannes. He'd have to fly from New York to London, or Paris, and then take a flight to Nice. It was about 30 minutes by taxi from Nice to Cannes. He worked out he could be there by Wednesday afternoon.

Chuck remembered that he'd texted Jake and now decided to call Jake, in London.

" Jake, It's Chuck, I'm on my way to Cannes, France, via Nice."

"I'd like to meet you in London on the way. Heathrow, Terminal 5, airside. Jake, can you arrange to get a ticket also same flight BA348 ? 17:10 London time tomorrow, arrives Cannes at 20:10 French time."

"Whoa, Chuck, Sure, Are you all right? where can we meet?"

"Doing fine, but life is somewhat hectic. How about the pub in the terminal? You know, the nice one, airside?"

"Huxleys? That's the less crowded one."

"Great. I'll see you there tomorrow. I'm in New York right now, so I'll be flying in during the day, on BA and then I'll make my way to the bar."

"Okay - I'll see you there, complete with a ticket!"

Huxley's

Chuck had flown back to London. He was in Heathrow Terminal 5, looking for the bar where he would meet Jake. Huxley's was busy. It was a replica pub, built into the 21st century fabric of the air terminal. It attempted to recreate a version of a gentrified London boozer.

"Jake!" called Chuck from across the bar. Jake noticed that Chuck was wearing one of his slightly green looking suits. Now was not the time to say anything.

"It's been a long time!" greeted Jake, "And I assume there's something 'unusual' involved?"

"Yes," said Chuck.

"What are you having?" asked Jake as he reached the bar and caught the eye of the bartender. She smiled at him with a twinkle in her eye.

"A water, please," said Chuck.

"Still or sparkling?" asked the bartender.

"Still," responded Chuck.

Jake looked across to Chuck.

"I need some help," said Chuck, "From people that are unknown. I seem to have got myself into a spot of trouble. There's been an incident and I am trying to put things right."

"Okay," said Jake, "I assume it's dangerous too, given that you are involved?"

"Yes," replied Chuck, "Some people have already been killed - but I don't want you to do anything dangerous, although your help could be a great game-changer in the current situation."

Chuck looked at Jake.

"Look, I'm going to trust you with this. I think you know me well enough to know I'm not making this up, although it might sound a little far-fetched."

"We'd better get a table then," smiled Jake. "And some pork scratchings".

Chuck began his story, "A few days ago I was sent to Egypt by the US Army. I know, I'm not officially anything to do with them now. I was contacted by the U.S.

The Square

Army's 1st Special Forces Operational Detachment-Delta (SFOD-D). It's a special unit of the U.S. government tasked with counterterrorist operations outside the United States."

"Sounds rather elite?" ventured Jake.

"Elite, deniable and deadly," answered Chuck, smiling.

"No clichés here, eh? I'm going to trust you with this information. I wouldn't usually tell anyone about this stuff, but I am going to need your help with something where I just can't go to the normal sources."

"Why is that?" asked Jake.

"Leaks," responded Chuck, "A major leak that makes me think some very senior people are involved in something that can create a global catastrophe."

"I hardly think that Bigsy, Clare and I can somehow fix this then?" smiled Jake.

"You are right, Jake. The point of getting you involved is to help me find some information that can then lead to unlocking what we need to do."

"My mission in Egypt was supposed to be fairly simple. The country has an inherent instability and I was to use the unrest to cover up my actual mission, which was to blow up a helicopter."

"Whoa," said Jake, "This is already getting dark."

"Literally. I'd been tasked with this as a black-op against terrorists. I was told that the truck carried something valuable to the U.S. but would be under attack from terrorists or mercenaries. They gave me co-ordinates to hit the helicopter before it could take out the truck."

"I'd been told that there were two parallel missions to take out two different trucks on different routes. I assumed they were carrying missiles, but I was wrong."

"They said they could give me the exact co-ordinates of the helicopter strike. I assumed that they obtained the intel from some kind of counterintelligence probe.

"I was to operate alone as a civilian, except I'd be a surprisingly well armed civilian. I was to have a selection of surface to air missiles at my disposal."

" I was given the intercept co-ordinates and told the truck would look like a petrol tanker. I was to use the weaponry at my disposal but explicitly it was non-American. I had to spend some time learning the controls on the Russian SAM launcher and on a Korean surface missile."

"I got this job on a 'non-refusal' basis. Uncle Sam has a few other facts about me that made this difficult to refuse. As an ex-Delta Force person I had the right credentials."

"Of course, if you are in the regular US Army you think that Delta Force has all the latest weaponry and equipment.

"The reality is that often, when someone like me is called in to action, the last thing required was a sophisticated American technology gloss on the operation. It's too much of a fingerprint when we need stealth. That is why I had to familiarise with foreign ordnance for this mission."

"I arrived in the locale for the operation in a 4 wheel Drive. A Nissan Patrol - the kind that everyone from the suburbs through to local gangsters and drug smugglers use.

"The vehicle I used looked slightly beaten up and in town would not be noticed. In the desert it was a typical vehicle too, and had plenty of space for the weaponry it currently carried.

"I never did find out who the other shooter was supposed to be, or even where the second convoy was heading. It's fairly standard in a black-op to know as little as possible."

"But you're telling me this now?" interrupted Jake,

"Yes, that mission is dead, but it is useful for you to have the context for what is about to happen next," Manners took another sip of his water.

"I guessed that the truck contained ordnance in transit. My guess was a very long-range missile. The popular theory is that any one of the Iraqis, Iranians, Libyans and Afganistanis would be seeking mischief with this sort of technology. It could be against a variety of nations, including the Americans, and all of Europe."

"How would the surveillance know about this?" asked Jake, "If major nation states can't find weapons of mass destruction then finding a single missile seems somewhat more far fetched?"

Manners nodded, "That's what I thought initially. A needle in a haystack. Unless there had been a tip-off. That's where this gets suspicious. If it really was a dangerous weapon, then in effect the Americans were helping it get to its destination.

Except it didn't because it was destroyed by the helicopter before I took the helicopter down.

"It turned out that whoever was shipping the consignment had tried to initialise it. Unsuccessfully."

"It had sent out a beacon pulse to say it was being tampered with. Like a silent alarm message which had found its way onto the internet and then been picked up at Langley."

"I'd speculated that this was no ordinary missile. The Pentagon showed a direct interest in this which made me think it was a 'bus-MIRV' which basically means long range nuclear capability."

"Bus doesn't sound very fast," queried Jake.

"These missiles are very fast. Ten times the speed of the fastest plane. They are launched into space and then triggered. The 'bus' means that one missile can contain multiple independent re-entry vehicles - that's warheads in plain English."

"That's why they are well scrutinised and tracked then?" commented Jake.

"Yes - the Pentagon can't keep up with all the smaller stuff nowadays. In Libya alone there's about 20,000 unaccounted surface-to-air missiles. They found an unguarded complex with 100,000 anti-tank mines as well. So, it's really the big stuff that gets their attention."

"My job was to shoot something at the missile to bring it to a halt. It could then be noisily recovered and put out of harm's way."

"Er - wouldn't your own missile cause it to explode or something?" asked Jake.

"Not a chance," answered Chuck, "Without the code sequences and arming commands, the whole missile is effectively made neutral. Don't get me wrong, there's very nasty stuff inside but the weapon is considered 'safe' until primed. They have to think of these things when they design the weapons or else it could all get very messy," explained Chuck.

"I was sitting in the Nissan, in the desert, pretty well concealed. I had some long-range digital binoculars and was scanning the area for other signs of people. All I could see was a single small car, but it was so far away that even with image enhancement I couldn't work out what it was doing."

"The next thing I heard was a high-pitched engine sound from the diesel truck. The sound reminded me of an American Army M923 transporter, but this was definitely a civilian rig.

Chuck continued, "I could also hear a low frequency sound which was getting closer. It was a helicopter"

"I looked up and could see the large attack helicopter. An Apache. Fully loaded. The chopper was following the truck and I noticed that the markings on the chopper had been painted out. I wondered initially if the helicopter was some sort of defence for the truck but realised that it had locked on to make an assault on the truck.

"The Apache fired one missile and the truck was obliterated. My orders were to take out anything associated with the truck and this now included the helicopter. I used a SAM to bring it down. I'd already got a laser and range lock from the digital binoculars.

The Square

"Two seconds and both the truck and the chopper were gone. The explosion from the truck had been huge, but non-nuclear. I was actually quite deaf at this point. In the far distance I could still see the other vehicle, which was now moving away, but it was out of any practical range for me to do more.

"So, did you leg it at this point?" asked Jake.

Chuck continued, "Strictly I could have left at this point. I was supposed to confirm that I'd taken out the truck, but it was plainly obvious even from around 3 clicks away.

"But I wanted to take a look because the helicopter wasn't playing by any normal rules.

"I had to look around the sky first, in case there was a backup plane, but if there had been it would have gone through very soon after the explosions. There was nothing, so I decided to edge the Nissan along the road towards the craters.

"I needed to move fast because even on this desert road there was traffic every 15-20 minutes.

"As I approached the helicopter I could see the extent of the damage. The SAM had destroyed the whole left side of the helicopter as well as the entire cockpit area. The remains of the rear part were clear and even its two remaining missiles were still attached but unexploded.

"The helicopter had been an AH64 Apache and this one was painted all over black and did not have normal markings except what looked like painted over squadron marking on the tail fin.

"I examined the remains of the intact side and then saw a painted over star. At "first I was thinking 'American' but the star was not in the right rotation - It looked Israeli.

"I scraped the paint. Under the black, the star was blue. I could see the surrounding circle which had also been painted out. I knew it would be white. It was.

"This was as Israeli helicopter, operating in Egypt. This broke all kinds of conventions and could only be assumed to be a covert operation."

"This is one twisted operation," said Jake, "No wonder you need someone with no background."

"I couldn't work out why an Israeli helicopter would be on fundamentally the same mission that I had been set. I also couldn't work out why they would take such extreme risks to attack in a stealth helicopter across an international border.

"I know I was doing this as a Delta Force gig, but only the Israeli equivalent Sayeret Matkal would be likely to do this.

The Square

"The difference was that the Americans had covered their tracks by using deniable resource, foreign weapons and local transport.

"The Israelis had just flown a repainted helicopter into the area. They must have expected to get away with their plan and to be able to escape quickly back to an international zone.

"I decided to fire another missile into the helicopter. Mainly to destroy the remains of the identification. I also thought it useful to mix in another type of armament to really mess things up, so I used the Korean surface missile. It was just a pop compared with the original explosions, but the tail section with the identity was pretty well obliterated.

"I also needed to check the minor remains of the truck, but was fairly sure they would provide very little information based upon the scale of destruction when the helicopter's own missile had been fired into the tanker.

"It took me another few minutes to get from the helicopter crash to the tanker's crater. There wasn't much to see. It had been a huge explosion, but still sub-nuclear. I looked around the site for evidence of the what had caused it, but there was nothing. I don't see how it could have been on board, but there was some kind of explosive being carried. Otherwise it doesn't add up. The missile from the Apache couldn't create as much devastation as it did, so my theory is that the truck included something to help things along."

"You're saying it was staged?" asked Jake.

"Staged isn't the word I would use, but it looks to me as if the intended result was to give the impression that something very big and powerful had been blown up."

"So they knew that someone was on to them?"

"I don't think the driver of the truck would have known, but someone must have leaked the information - and in more than one direction too. The destruction also was not consistent with a large missile being blown up. It makes me think that truck was carrying something else."

"So, they wanted everyone to think that the truck had been blown up?"

"Yes - and the fact that they'd got the Americans and the Israelis onto it suggests that they didn't want to take any chances."

"So, then what?" asked Jake.

"I had to get out of the area. The road where it happened was pretty out of the way. It ran parallel to another busier road but was about 10 miles to the south. The amount of noise and smoke would attract attention and only give a few minutes before others would come for a look. And then the police and military.

"As it happens, for me it was 'Mission Accomplished' - the truck was gone, it's just that there was a spare helicopter downed as well. My Nissan was completely unscathed in all of this, so I headed along the roadway from Cairo and then turned down another small road back towards the main highway and across to the other highway."

"Wouldn't someone want additional support in the area?" asked Jake.

"Too risky," answered Chuck, "If you think about it, the truck was supposed to be travelling under cover. No-one was supposed to know about it. The Americans could hardly appear in the area unless everyone pointed a finger towards them and as for the Israelis, forget it. One disguised helicopter was the absolute limit."

"Yes," said Jake, nodding, "showing up just after a massive missile fight wouldn't be the brightest move."

"And as it was, I didn't see anyone approaching the crash by road, as I headed back to the main route. But I guess they would have come from the Cairo direction. Any normal civilian would probably want to give it a wide berth - either because it was insurgents of some kind, or simply because they were in a hurry and didn't want to get stuck in a traffic hold-up."

Jake nodded.

"So, what do you want me or us to do?" he asked again

Diversion

"It's something you are very good at," Chuck replied, "A diversion, while I do something else. I am trying to recover something for our Governments. To be honest, I am trying to recover something despite our governments."

Jake smiled. A diversion would be fun.

"What kind of diversion?" he asked. "And why is it despite the government?"

"It's best you don't know too much about what I will be doing, but whilst I'm doing it, it would be great if you can help the people we are working with look the other way."

"I'll level with you. My colleague James has had his partner kidnapped. They are after some codes and want to arrange a trade."

"The captors could play nice or could act up rough. The intention is to show them that I have back-up with me."

The Square

"We need to go to a bar in Cannes, hand over the codes and walk out with James' partner Léa."

"You'll be my driver. We'll also have someone from the Embassy to add colour and texture inside the handover."

"How will they know the codes are genuine?"

I guess they will have a boffin along," answered Chuck, "someone that can test the codes somehow."

Will anyone get hurt during this?" asked Jake.

"No, they shouldn't. If we do this right, then no-one should even know what has happened until it is too late to do anything at all."

"Chuck, why won't you use the normal security services for this?" asked Jake.

"It's delicate," said Chuck, "This is one situation where I need to ensure there are no leaks of information and frankly that no-one else knows what I'm doing. I know I can trust you for this."

Chuck looked Jake in the eye, "But I do need to know that you'll be prepared to do this."

"Chuck, you've assured us that we won't be in danger. Of course we will help you."

Jake nodded. It wasn't so different from the last time he'd been with Chuck. Nothing was really what it seemed, and this was a typical extension.

"Don't you ever get confused with all of these parallel realities?" asked Jake.

Chuck smiled, "We both know how it is," he replied, "if it was too simple then everyone would do it."

"I've set up a fake conference number to control the operation. Like a dial-in conference call. We are going to leak the number to the people at the meeting. We will need some voices on the line to sound like it is a major operation. They need to think that you've got the phone for that purpose and are under orders."

"Okay, so that's where Bigsy and Clare come in? Making air chatter?"

"Precisely," said Chuck. "To bulk out the operation with voices on the line. We'll want them to think they had better play nice with us."

"Okay, I'd better get on to Bigsy; get him to come up with some sound effects,"

- .... . / .... .- -. -.. --- ...- . .-.

Léa's handover had been arranged. James made his way to the Carlton Beach Club along the Croisette. He could see Chuck Manners and someone else already there, sitting at the bar.

"Hi James," called Chuck, "This is Jake, he'll be joining us for the occasion."

Jake nodded; the sleek setting of the jet-set exclusive club seemed an incongruous place to meet for the handover.

"And over there is Oliver, from the British Consulate," he gestured to another table where Oliver sat, flamboyantly listening to a radio communication on an earpiece.

James also noticed a small group of the people he had met in New York and that had then seen him at Café L'Ondine a day or so ago in Cannes.

Oliver's earpiece was quite loud and he could hear sound leakage from it as it changed modes.

James adjusted his own earpiece, which also had the running commentary from further voices which sounded as if a full stake-out was in progress.

At that moment, he noticed a sleek powerboat curving its way across the bay. He realised it was planning to dock on the jetty and he realised that this was where Léa was held.

Ever so slowly he moved forward towards the end of the jetty, holding a machined briefcase in his right hand. He knew it contained the codes which Chuck had painstakingly retrieved with the assistance of Robert Alton. The difference was that the case was now a regular one, without a special electronic lock incorporated.

Someone stepped from the launch. It was a bespectacled man, in a grey tee-shirt and shorts. He was carrying a small laptop and gestured to James to hand over the case.

Chuck stood at that moment and James could hear the sound in his earpiece get louder.

"Okay, here's the case, now hand over Léa," he said.

"I need to validate the codes first," said the man. He flipped open the case and took a sheet of paper from it. He opened the laptop and started to type in something. James could not see what he was doing.

"I'm using the validation suite to check the codes are correct," said the man. There was a pause as he continued typing.

"Yes," he said eventually, " These codes all pass the validation tests."

He signalled to back to the launch and Léa appeared on deck, held by two men in suits.

"You can release her now," said James. Chuck looked across to the man with the laptop.

The Square

"That way we can let your scientist friend go," said Chuck, grasping the arm of the man with the laptop.

"Okay, Okay," said one of the men holding Léa, "We are releasing her now."

The boat rocked against the jetty as Léa walked towards its exit. Chuck moved his arm into his jacket. The radio chatter in James' ear continued.

Léa was now close to the bar in the Beach Club and James put his arm around her, moving her towards the exit. Jake was sitting in a car on the Croisette as the two of them approached. Chuck moved towards the boat with the man with the laptop.

"He can go now," said Chuck, "This should be an end of it."

The man on the powerboat nodded, "Yes, your team can go now."

Chuck walked backwards towards the exit from the Beach Club. Oliver stood and took a couple of photographs. The radio chatter continued. Chuck could hear Jake revving the engine of the rental car as he made his way along the Croisette.

"Mission accomplished," he said to Oliver. He gestured to a second car parked on the Croisette opposite the Beach Club. "That's ours, " he said, "We are off to the heliport and then flying to Marseille. Hit it, Oliver."

Oliver looked over to the black Mercedes E-Class and jumped into the driver's seat.

"You've done well," said Chuck, "The least we could do is give you a fast route back to Marseilles."

At the heliport, they regrouped. Chuck could see that James and Léa were delighted. Chuck announced, "We are going to head for Marseilles. It is harder to follow us there. And I've arranged in the UK for Léa and James to be put up in a somewhat secure location, until the dust from all of this subsides."

"Good," said Jake, "Now we have everyone back together,"

"Yes," said Chuck, "but the bad guys have the priming codes for the toxins."

Chuck could see Oliver taking rapidly to someone on the earpiece.

Oliver soon announced," That was Robert Alton. He confirms if we bring James and Léa in he will provide them with secure cover.

Truck One

Ghali Yassim was thinking back to the first news of the destroyed truck. Most of the conversation was recorded and he was playing it back for the fifth time, trying to find any new meaning in it.

"Something has happened," said Ghali Yassim. "We have lost contact with the first truck."

The destruction of the truck had been fast. It had created a lot of noise, even more because of the subsequent explosion in mid-air of the attack helicopter.

Al Aktar had used their normal procedures to send the two trucks out by different routes.

In practice, Al Aktar had no idea about what had been happening or that they were down to one consignment. This would change in the next couple of hours, when the truck missed its call-in time.

The other truck containing the second consignment was still on its longer journey, to London, England.

Al Aktar's control centre was in the desert along a trail that branched from Egypt 75, which led to Abu Simbel. The makeshift centre included a neglected airstrip. They could land a medium sized plane, had a helicopter port and also several tin sheds which could be used to store trucks and other vehicles and armaments. They were also within easy reach of the main Abu Simbel Airport, which gave them access to main routes.

Al Aktar devised a safety protocol for the trucks, to call in at two-hour intervals to allow an update of their position to be tracked. The next checkpoint time arrived, and the London-bound truck called in and noted that all was okay.

There was no message from the other truck and there was then an attempt to call it directly from the radio-masted control system. They left it another thirty minutes and then tried to call the truck direct.

There was no response.

They would do these another three times and at the end of that period they would assume that something had happened to the consignment.

The Square

Their control centre was already checking the television channels for any reports of trucks being stopped, unusual road conditions or worse, but there was nothing.

"Send up the helicopter, along the route; we need to know", and a few minutes later the helicopter departed, creating a small swirl of sand as it moved skyward. It covered the first part of the route in a few minutes, and soon radioed back with the news of the wreckage of the truck but also of an adjacent helicopter wreck and some new air traffic approaching the wreck.

"They may think they have stopped us,"said Mehdi

Ed Adams

PART

TWO

THREE WEEKS AGO

Kent

"The hop gardens turn gracefully towards me presenting regular avenues of hops in rapid flight, then whirl away."

Charles Dickens, rail journey through Kent

Ashford

Ashford, Kent, Channel Tunnel train station: It was the stopping point for the white van containing the cases being driven from the dilapidated houses in Hoxton, London. The driver of the van and his passenger had been hired to convey the cases to Ashford, where they would be swapped into a large truck for the rest of their journey.

The October rain from London seemed to have swept across the whole of the south of England. As Alan drove and Dave sat in the passenger seat, they talked to begin with, but then fell silent as they each were caught in their own thoughts before the drop-off. This was an expensive piece of ferrying for their clients, but there was always a chance that something would cut up rough when they got to the drop-off point. They'd been warned not to bring anyone else along and had decided that they had little choice but to obey. They had worked for the same Arabs before on a couple of smaller deals and had found them to be reliable and to always pay without asking questions.

Alan, the driver, and Dave, his passenger, knew that they were moving the cases to another vehicle and drove to the appointed rendezvous. They were punctual and noted a huge Scania articulated truck already parked in the lay-by behind a black Mercedes with blacked out back windows. Two men with middle eastern looks and beards were standing by the cab of the truck. One wore a black tee shirt, the other was in a green jacket. A third man was sitting in the truck's cab, which had Polish number plates on the cab and what looked like Dutch plates on the trailer.

Dave jumped from the van onto a slightly crunchy road surface in the lay-by. As he looked around, he realized that he didn't know the men who he was being asked to meet.

"Guys, we're here", called out Dave, "Who is in charge?" as he looked around. With a whirring sound, a back window in the Merc ran down and a third Arabic looking face peered out. "Do you have the cases?" he asked.

"Six cases," answered Dave. "Everything's here!"

"Let's check," responded the guy in the black tee shirt, as he pulled the door of the van open and pulled the first case forward. The second man pulled open a large holdall, like a military kitbag. As the first man opened the cases, he handed the envelopes individually to the second man, and they counted them into the holdall.

The Square

Despite the rain, the envelopes were counted as they were transferred. Six cases with ten envelopes in each. "There's only 59", called the Arab with the black tee shirt.

"Are you sure?", said the man in the green jacket, "Count them again".

The van driver and his passenger looked at each other.

They had worked together a long time, and neither of them would double cross the other.

"We don't have any other envelopes", said the driver. The three Arabs briefly conferred.

"There is an envelope missing", repeated the Arab with the black tee shirt. The Arab in the black Mercedes called out something else. The driver and passenger looked at one another, worried now that something bad was about to happen.

"You have two days," said the black tee shirt, "We don't care what has happened, but you will find the missing package - it is essential that we retrieve it. As good faith we will still give you your money, minus fifty percent. You will get the rest minus ten per cent when you provide the missing package. Please do not fail, it will be very unpleasant for you and your families. You have forty-eight hours. We meet again here at the same time. Do not fail and do not think you can walk away from this commitment."

The Arab in the green jacket moved to the trunk of the Mercedes and lifted a briefcase, which he carried to Dave. He briefly flicked it open.

"You'll find half of the money here," he said and flipped the two catches of the case to reveal the money. There seemed to be a lot of cash in the briefcase and Dave briefly flicked through a couple of the stacks and noticed that they all looked like used notes too.

"Thank you for this first payment," he said and scooped the case so that he and Alan could move back to their van. He nodded to Alan, who swung back onto the passenger seat. They started the engine and pulled back out onto the busy road.

Dave and Alan had just received £300,000, which was exactly half of the £600,000 they had expected. It was still a considerable sum, and they knew it would get very nasty if they tried to argue about the rest. They were really small-time criminals, and the job they had been given was essentially the delivery of the six cases. They had considered this easy money but were now concerned that things were getting complicated.

"Dave, do you think that the drunk could have taken an envelope?", Alan asked, as they thought over what had happened.

The Square

They had been professional about counting the envelopes when they had been given them in the first place and had kept the six cases under watch at all times except briefly when they were transferring them from the hide-out to the current van.

"The only time we didn't have the full set in sight was when we were clearing up at the lock-up," said Dave. "The envelope is either there, or one of those squatters has it," he said referring to the drunken guy who had been loitering at the squat.

"Okay," said Dave, "We'll go back to the lockup, check that we've not done something stupid and find the guy that probably has!"

Back to the lock-up

Dave and Alan drove straight from Ashford back to central London. They were both furious about what had happened. The original deal had seemed sweet. All they had been expected to do was collect some cases and move them.

They had checked the cases when they collected them and somehow had lost one of the packages along the way. The only clue that anything was wrong was when they had met the drunk during the loading of the cases into the van. Neither Dave nor Alan believed that they were being double crossed and they both believed it was an accident. Either they had really misplaced a package (unlikely) or the drunken tramp had somehow stolen one. If it was the tramp, they would find him and ask him where the package had now been taken.

The next morning, at seven o'clock, they pulled the van onto a pavement around two blocks from the squat. They would walk the last part of the way to the lock-up garage and the deserted houses, to find the tramp who would probably still be asleep.

First they checked back to the original yard where they had parked the van.

"There's nothing here," said Dave, "although you can see where the tramp was laying on the ground".

Alan nodded. He had brought a small holdall with him. It only contained a few workman's tools, but his intention was to get the information from the tramp under any circumstances. The Arabs now had half of the money he was owed but had also threatened him and his family if they did not return the envelope. And the irony was, he still didn't know what the goods actually were.

They climbed a small wall into the area behind the yard and looked around for the tramp. Ben had a normal sleeping area, and it was in a different house from Gerald, so they kept some distance and some slight security because of this.

The two men had first spotted Ben's house and lifted the broken door inwards to enter the house. There was a crash of timber as they did this. Both Ben and Gerald had learnt that causal intruders usually walked in through the doors and so had piled some noisy items against the door ready to fall, as a form of primitive burglar alarm. Ben was in deep sleep, an after effect of cheap cider, when Dave and Alan found him. They woke him and he groggily asked who they were, then recognising them as the men who he had startled the previous day by the van.

"What do you want?", coughed Ben, as the first man started to hold him to the wall.

"You know what we want", answered Alan glaring at Ben, "You took something from us yesterday - we want it back".

Ben looked confused, "You hit me yesterday, but I had not taken anything", he replied, "I don't know what you want!"

Dave and Alan looked at one another. "This will get very painful for you if you don't tell us the truth!" responded Dave, as Alan opened the zipper on the holdall revealing a few tools including a plumber's wrench. Ben looked at the bag, and its contents, and could see also some knives and a hacksaw.

"I promise you," said Ben, "I don't know what you are talking about!"

The noise had created a commotion in the house, but Gerald, in the next house, had been alerted even by the first crash when the men had entered through the front door of the house. He had slipped quietly in through a window and could now see what was happening. He quickly realised that the two men were trying to find the missing envelope which he had stolen from one of the cases. He could see that Ben was in a lot of trouble.

Gerald decided to find the envelope and try to return it to the two men. He crept out of the house via the same window and then stealthily moved to his hiding place. He considered substituting the strange metal container for something else from his collection, but then realised that he would not want another visit from the same men, looking for him. He just wanted this visit to be over.

He slipped back to the window and could see one of the men placing the plumber's wrench around Ben's left hand as if to crush it. Ben was screaming, but still seemed relatively unscathed. Gerald decided to take a gamble. No-one had seen him, and the two men did not know his appearance. He would throw the envelope into the room and run away and hide. If that was all the men wanted, this could be the end of it.

He took a corner of the envelope, briefly stood, threw the envelope which flew directly towards the cluster of three men in the room and then turned and ran. Gerald was thinking to himself that this was the opposite of brave, but at least it gave Ben a chance and whatever was in the bag was untraceable to him.

Dave and Alan turned as the brown padded envelope slid across the floor. They couldn't make out where it had come from but assumed it had been thrown from one of the windows. "Is this the envelope?" Dave asked. "If it is, we are out of here!"

Alan looked at the package. "It's been opened," he said.

"I'm going to check what is inside". He slid the small cylinder into his hand. "Is this what we have been carrying?" he asked Dave.

"It looks special enough." replied Dave, realising that neither of them knew the original contents so this was a gamble.

Then looking back to Ben, "You are very lucky," he said to Ben, then punching him in the stomach, causing him to arch double and slide to the floor.

"C'mon," said Dave, "Let's go".

They walked out through the front door and then nonchalantly along the road back to their parked van. They would lay low until their second meeting with the Arabs.

Gerald saw the two men leave the house, he watched them as they walked back to their van. He noted the number. He would know if this van was back in the neighbourhood. Then he walked back to check on Ben.

Ben was still on the floor when he reached him. He was the worse for wear, but not a lot worse than he had been some nights when he had drunk too much cider.

The Square

"You were very lucky!", said Gerald, "They seem to have got what they needed!".

Ben nodded. "Have you got any cider?" he asked.

Containment

This time, Alan and Dave took a small car back to Ashford. It would be less conspicuous than the van and also gave them an element of surprise if they needed to make a reconnaissance of the area before meeting the Arabs. They arrived an hour early by the lay-by but kept driving as if they were heading somewhere else.

There were several large trucks parked and a couple of cars, but nothing as conspicuous as the black Mercedes from the last visit. They tried to guess the type of vehicle which would be waiting, but there was nothing obvious, like a large SUV. The trucks themselves had mainly foreign registrations, but this was perfectly normal for an area very close to the Channel Tunnel Europort.

They continued to another lay-by, a smaller one with a small snack-bar and here they simply waited until close to the appointed time. Then, with Alan driving, they crossed the road and headed back to the meeting point.

As they arrived, they could see a couple of long articulated lorries and a couple of vans. They pulled in and Dave stood up out of the car. No-one looked towards him and he decided to walk up and down the lay-by, ostentatiously banging his arms around his body, as if he was cold. This would attract oblique attention and should make it easy for the people he was to exchange with to make contact.

There was a noise behind him, and he looked around. A motorcyclist on a powerful Honda had just pulled in behind him.

The guy on the motorcycle called out, "Follow me", and revved his engine.

Dave ran slowly back to the car and exchanged a few words with Alan. They looked at each other; if this was the meeting, no-one had said anything about it being elsewhere. They decided they had really no option but to follow the biker. They didn't think anyone else could have known about the meeting.

The biker pulled out onto the road and headed back towards London, the direction they had originally come from. At the first major junction, the bike pulled off and then headed along a road to the left. They followed him and soon found themselves in a small industrial estate. In the distance they could see a couple of cars, including a Mercedes like the one that had met them the first time.

With some relief they pulled up at a small Portakabin adjacent to where the Mercedes was parked. The motor cyclist dismounted and gestured.

"Bring it with you", he said.

They looked at each other again, and Alan nodded. He had the envelope in a large concealed poacher's pocket of the Barbour waxed jacket he was wearing. They stepped from the car and followed the motor cyclist into the Portakabin. The biker had removed his helmet as he walked towards the Portakabin and Alan and Dave could see he was middle eastern, but not any of the people he had met before. They walked into the Portakabin, which was essentially one large room with some sort of annex.

Inside there were two other people, both seated. "Welcome", said the biker, "Hand over the item and you are free to go". "So why did you bring us here?", asked Dave.

"Containment," said one of the seated men. "If you have co-operated, then there will be no problem, if you have not, then we have some privacy".

Alan called out, "I am going to reach into my coat to get it".

The Square

One of the two men seated stood up as Alan said this.

"Slowly", he said.

Alan obeyed and gently took the item from his pocket and placed it on the desk in front of the still seated man. The biker reached over and picked up the envelope and very gently shook the contents onto the desk. The metallic tube rolled momentarily and then stopped. The three strangers all looked at one another. The biker said, "Okay, you can go".

Alan said, "Our money? you still owe us half..."

The biker responded, "You have your lives, go now, before we change our minds".

Alan and Dave decided this was probably their safest option and moved towards the door. They had still made £300,000 for a relatively small amount of delivery work. They hurried for the door, and then jumped back in their car to make their exit.

"I think we have just been very lucky," said Dave.

Back inside the Portakabin, the three occupants watched as Dave and Alan drove away.

"Well done, Mohammed," said Robert Alton, "That was excellent, now what have we actually retrieved?".

Muhammad smiled. If it had not been for Karen's discovery the previous day, they would not be this far along with their investigation. And now the extra SI6 men outside of the Portakabin had a tracker bug on Dave and Alan's car, so they could track them and pull them in at any time, if they needed more information.

. . .

There was a moment of silence in the Portakabin after Dave and Alan had left. Then Robert Alton emerged from the back office.

"So, we have a chemical vial full of Lord knows what," he started, "and a consignment bound from the Eurolink by truck to the Middle East. We will need to intercept the truck and retrieve the contents."

"In the meantime, we need to get the current sample analysed by a safe chemical facility. I suspect we need to send this to Porton Down, it could have anything inside."

At this time Alton suspected it was something very unpleasant but didn't know for sure. He could tell by the container that this was not something to be idly opened.

"We should pull in Andy and Dave," he said, looking at the evidence in front of him.

Andy and Dave were barely two miles from the Portakabin when they ran into the roadblock. It was a full military situation, and they knew better than to to try to drive past it. A single soldier was asking them to stop, but they could see other firepower immediately to the side and behind him.

"What seems to be the problem?" asked Alan. "Please just step out of the vehicle", came the reply, "and put your hands on your head."

Both Dave and Alan exited the car. They were frightened now and not sure if the soldiers were real or another part of some kind of deception. But the guns looked real enough so now was not the time to argue.

"Please step into the van," instructed one of the soldiers, "We will need to ask you a few questions."

Dave and Alan were transported to the large secure SI6 facility where the Arabs were under detention. They were taken to a different area for cross examination.

The key information required was a description of the vehicle used to transport the other vials. Alan was able to be very helpful here, because he had written down the number of the first truck when they had met.

"Here's the information." he said, handing over a small notebook. He had taken several notes during the job, more as insurance in case anything was to go wrong, but he had not expected things to develop the way the last few hours had been progressing.

"We do have a truck registration", he said, "Its Polish and the number is STO 792" he added. "I wrote it down when we transferred the first set of envelopes to the Arabs."

"And when was that?" asked his interrogator, smiling.

"Er, look, we are just drivers. This was a well-paid van delivery, that's all," continued Dave, "The original job was to get some packets from London to Ashford in the van. Somehow one went missing and we had to go back for it. The first exchange was yesterday. We were given 24 hours to put it right, so we just drove back to London, found the missing package and returned."

Dave looked earnestly at his interrogator. "Really, that's all I know."

The interrogator looked at Dave. The room was wired for sound and vision. He said to Dave and the cameras, "Okay, I'm going outside for a few minutes. Is there anything we can get you?"

"What, like a coffee or something," asked Dave, "Am I going to be here much longer?"

"I'm afraid so," answered the interrogator, "Actually, I don't think you'd last very long outside at the moment."

Dave looked concerned, "And what about Alan?" he asked, "When can I see him?"

The Square

The interrogator looked at Dave. "I'll see if I can get you some coffee," he replied.

Outside, Robert Alton and Mohammed had already compared the stories from Dave and Alan. They were almost word perfect, except that Alan didn't know the truck registration.

"Small time." said Alton, "And they seem to be telling the truth."

Mohammed nodded, "The truck registration is a lucky breakthrough."

"Yes, we are on to it," replied Alton, "Although, they will have done a switch by now, either in the tunnel or as soon as they got to France."

Ed Adams

RIGHT NOW

Strong women

Take this pink ribbon off my eyes
I'm exposed
And it's no big surprise
Don't you think I know
Exactly where I stand
This world is forcing me
To hold your hand

'Cause I'm just a girl, little ol' me
Well don't let me out of your sight
Oh, I'm just a girl, all pretty and petite
So don't let me have any rights
Oh, I've had it up to here!

Gwen Stefani

Elisa Solomons

Jake had decided to take Clare and Bigsy along to the next meeting with Chuck. He knew Chuck would expect this and it would anyway be easier to remember the complexities of the next stage of what they were being tasked to do.

"Why on earth has Chuck picked such a busy bar to meet?" said Bigsy. They were on a corner of Sloane Square in a bar heaving with an early evening crowd.
"It was my idea actually," said Jake, "I thought we could meet here and then immediately go to somewhere else. It reduces the chance we are being followed."

"That's not such a bad plan," said Clare, "I'm having flashbacks to our scrapes in Zurich."

"Yes - we just need to find Chuck and then we are on our way,"

The Square

At that moment, Chuck appeared leaving the doorway of an adjacent building. He was with someone else, a slim, attractive woman in a neat dark business suit. She was carrying a small bag and also a laptop case. Chuck appeared to be carrying a bulky camouflage coloured rucksack.

"Hi Chuck," called Jake. "Great to meet again and punctual as ever, you remember Clare and Bigsy?"
"Indeed, I do and hello everyone, let me introduce my colleague Elisa to you all".

They each shook hands and were about to find a way into the busy bar when Jake said, "Let's move. I know a great pastry shop nearby."

Bigsy smiled. He was already thinking about whether to have Black Forest Gateau or Double Chocolate Dream Gateau.

"I thought we could be more - er - alone - in the cafe."

Chuck nodded.

"Lead on."

"It's less than five minutes walk from here, across the Square."

Bigsy led the way, and the others fell into step. Clare chatted to Elisa about the area, and the fairly fancy shops close by. Bigsy and Chuck chatted about Stuttgart, which was where Chuck had been staying just before the call from London.

Jake looked behind as they walked, and then to left and right. There didn't appear to be anyone following. He noticed Chuck doing something similar.

Within a few minutes they had arrived at the patisserie. "Not your most likely meeting place to hatch a plot?" said Jake.

"There's no place out of bounds," smiled Chuck.

They pulled two small four-person tables together, ordered some coffees and talked.

"Everyone, this is Elisa, or should I say Doctor Elisa Solomons. We have known one another for many years. When the recent situation that I've described to Jake came up, I thought I'd ask Elisa if she had any insights."

Elisa smiled, "I have known Chuck since a time almost ten years ago when he helped me with a big problem. I worked in a chemical facility in North Carolina. Unknown to me, I was being targeted for some retribution based upon another scientist that had died. It is crazy, but there's another kind of brain drain based around eliminating some scientists considered being working on things that could be classed as advanced weaponry. Someone had blown up an Iranian nuclear scientist with a car bomb. He wasn't the first to be killed. Maybe the fourth. The response each time was to look for a victim. I didn't realise it, but I had become a target."

"Why?" asked Clare, "What do you do?"

"What I did wasn't in any way dangerous. I was trying to find stabilisers for some forms of viral disease. It was mis-communicated that I was working on neuro-toxins. Then I met Chuck. It was at an airport actually, in a line waiting for a delayed plane. He started chatting politely to me and as we both had time to kill, I didn't initially think much of it."

Chuck looked serious faced as Elisa explained her story. "Then he took me to one side and explained who he was. That he worked for the US Government and that he had been tasked with protecting me. I didn't believe it at first - thought he was some kind of crank," she smiled across the table to him and he smiled back, "but he had a dossier of information about me and also a set of intelligence reports about the other scientists that had been assassinated."

"I was pretty freaked out by the whole thing, but then he said he would make the problem go away. I thought there's no way he can stop a determined set of assassins from targeting me and I couldn't face long-term protection."

She paused and looked across to Chuck again. "Chuck's plan was simple."

"Let me guess," interrupted Clare, "He would have you killed, anyway?"

Elisa nodded, "I can see you all know Chuck. That was his plan. He had located a cell supposed to be tracking me and would let them think they had blown me up."

"Wasn't that kind of 'elaborate' to achieve?" asked Jake.

"It was," interrupted Chuck, "But Elisa is a precious asset."

"Melodrama aside, Chuck is right," said Elisa, "the research I do is for the right and ethical reasons. It also means I am one of a few people who understand some man-made neurotoxins created in the era of the Cold War and beyond. Most of it is illegal now, but the USA and a few other countries like to have people around that can fast path the route to antidotes."

"Elisa is one of those people," said Chuck, "So, although she was being targeted for the wrong reasons, she was still someone we would very much want to protect."
"Cutting a long story short," continued Elisa, "I was then blown up in a very messy car bomb explosion whilst travelling through Nigeria."

"It was a perfect cover story," said Chuck, "and removed Elisa from circulation."

"You weren't called Elisa then?" asked Clare.

"No," answered Elisa. "The problem with all of this is that I had to get a complete new identity and move to another country. I chose U.K. And I don't think anyone else knows what you've just been told."

Chuck nodded, "I was the only person permitted to know Elisa's ongoing identity and also became the link should there ever be a need to call on Elisa's services to support a toxin related problem."

"So why now?" asked Jake.

"There's been some developments," replied Chuck. "The missile I was hunting wasn't a missile."

"No, it was some form of neuro-toxin being carried in a truck," replied Elisa.

"How so?" asked Clare.

"For the first time since my demise in the car bombing, someone has asked to speak to me via Chuck. It can only mean one thing. There's a neuro toxin agent on the loose."
"This is all sounding too Science Fiction!" said Jake.

"This is what I've put together so far," said Chuck.

"Firstly, I'm asked to visit the desert. To destroy a missile. I try, but someone gets there first."

"Secondly, When I look at the transport, the explosion is way too large to be from a dormant missile."

"Third, the people that blow up the truck are from Israel."

"Fourth, the whole thing is ultra-sensitive."

"Fifth, I get asked to restart a link to Elisa."

"This is what we think has happened," continued Elisa.

"Someone created a toxin; it's too dangerous to keep. It gets destroyed, except, someone keeps a small quantity on file for the records."

"The toxin gets stolen or released and everyone sees how dangerous it is. It gets passed along to be destroyed, but somehow gets stolen in the process. They call me to help them figure out how to contain and destroy it."

"So did the truck in the desert have a missile on it?" asked Jake.

"I was told it did when I was out there. The truck was carrying a set of disabled neurotoxin canisters."

"So why not just let the various government agencies clean this up?" asked Jake.

"That's what I thought initially," answered Chuck, "but then I realised that there was a power play in all of this.

My guess is that some of the people involved in this see the toxin as a form of leverage. Someone I was speaking to from SI6 said that the toxin can be deployed from a MIRV."

"Eh?" asked Clare.

"Yes, a Multiple Independently-targetable Reentry Vehicle or MIRV - that's exactly what we are dealing with, and what I originally thought was on the transport." answered Chuck.

"They were originally developed in the early '60s to permit a missile to deliver multiple nuclear warheads to different targets. We used to test them in the desert, around Nevada. Not just our own ones, we also had some captured Russian ones.

"For instance, a Russian MIRV missile could carry up to 16 warheads, each in a separate re-entry vehicle. Warheads on MIRV missiles can be released from the missile at different speeds and in different directions. Some MIRV missiles can hit targets as far as 1,500 kilometres apart.

Then we had some land-based ones too, they were particularly destabilizing, because it was a game of cat and mouse to find them.

The common consensus was that development of MIRV technology was difficult. A combination of large missiles, small warheads, accurate guidance, and a complex mechanism for releasing warheads sequentially during flight.

That's why it is likely that the truck would have both the missile and some warheads on board. It would also explain the absolute intensity of the strike by the helicopter, to destroy absolutely everything.

"I'm afraid that points to one thing, said Elisa, "That the warheads were not conventional, not even fissile. It points to them being biological."

"What?" said Bigsy, "So the truck was pulling a set of biological warheads across the desert, the sort that can be used in a MIRV?"

"Yes, " answered Elisa, "And the individual warheads will be deadly by themselves. It becomes a case of using a different delivery mechanism."

"That's right," said Chuck, "We used to test both long range delivery and asymmetric delivery, using something like a truck-bomb."

"The truck bomb was supposed to be a poor man's cruise missile, but trust me, it was effective."

"If we envisage one of these small units in a truck and then it driven to a specific location, then anything could happen?" asked Clare.

"Yes," said Elisa, "But for one safety mechanism. Usually these weapons are digitally encoded, to fail safe. That means that inside them is a safety component. If the canister is tampered, the safety explodes and destroyed the payload. Similarly, without priming, these warheads can't be detonated. The same safety mechanisms cut in to destroy the warhead content."

"Yes, ever since the 1960s, Failsafe has been a big deal with the more advanced weapons," added Chuck, "Remember the dead-man's handle on trains or the cut-off on lawnmowers? It's the same idea."

"Yes," although one of these would mow an awful lot of grass if in the wrong hands," added Jake.

"So what is this about now?" asked Bigsy, "Leverage?"

"Yes, I can see that," answered Clare. "He who controls the missing weapon has a lot of power."

"Yes, the ability to make all kinds of demands," answered Chuck, "Now I don't want to be all self-righteous about this but I'm fearful if we don't put an end to this then there could some serious power brokering from unpredictable sources."

"Do you think the US and UK governments are mixed up with this?" asked Clare.

"Almost certainly, and for their own ends," answered Chuck, "Hence the need for stealth."

"So, here's my supposition," continued Elisa.

"When I lived in Tel-Aviv, I used to work with the Israeli government on virus research. The funding provided by the government to this was exceptional and it was a great place to work."

"My own research was purely medical-related and was looking for advances in immunology. I knew many of the other scientists and although we didn't talk directly about the classified material, it was obvious that there was another group working on munitions style virus product. - A reverse take on scientists that build and those that destroy. This was science to kill and science looking for an antidote."

"At some point one of the labs was closed down completely. We were told it was electrical problems, but everyone knew it was a toxin related closedown. The whole lab system had to be sealed off. I wasn't directly involved in any of it but several people I knew were and they looked pretty scared about what had taken place."

"And then I noticed that the team were all transferred away. It was overnight, and they just disappeared. I have not heard from any of them since."

"So how did this link to the threat to you?" asked Clare.

"It didn't," answered Elisa.

"But I did spend some time thinking about what seemed to have happened."

"They were making something nasty and then disappeared?" asked Clare, glancing towards Chuck.

Elisa continued, "Clare's right. They were working on a type of biological weapon. Using some form of airborne viral carrier - which is actually more difficult than it sounds. Let me explain."

"A virus is a piece of genetic information a bit like the way DNA works. It is packaged in an envelope of proteins or lipids sometimes including sugars. Viruses cannot live by themselves but must be able to quickly get into a plant or animal cells to survive."

"These viruses use the energy metabolism and the biosynthetic machinery of the host cell to replicate themselves. It is like they harness the existing biological machinery of their host"

Jake interjected, "Like a sort of parasite?"

Elisa nodded, "It's similar, during the phase of replication inside the host cell - we scientists call it a eukaryotic cell - a virus makes a copy of its RNA or DNA and from that copy duplicates itself."

"It's quite a clever process, because it also makes extra enzymes so that it can build a protective envelope while it is working."

"I know about DNA, what's RNA?", asked Clare.

"If you know about DNA, you'll remember it has a special structure - the 'double helix' - RNA, which stands for Ribonucleic acid is a similar type of molecule, but without the double helix structure. It's used by living things to make more protein and to keep DNA structures called ribosomes regulated."

"Whoa - here comes the science part!" joked Jake.

"Jake!", Clare jabbed Jake in the ribs and looked towards Elisa to continue.

"Yes, there is some more science," said Elisa,

"The three-dimensional structures of RNA molecules show architectural motifs exploited for the design of artificial RNA nanomaterials.

"Put simply, at present , scientists can only create RNA objects in certain shapes. One of these at a tiny size of 2.2 Ångstrom is a square-shaped nanoobject made entirely of double-stranded RNA.

The Square

The RNA square is comprised of 100 residues and self-assembles from four copies each of two oligonucleotides of 10 and 15 bases length.

You have to imagine the programmed self-assembly of RNA squares from complex mixtures of corner units to build the RNA square as a combinatorial platform. It's that square shape that can regulate the nerve agent.

In other words, the same biological machine that can replicate nerve agent can also hold it in check?" asked Bigsy.

"Yes, that's why they call the agents tertiaries. A base agent. A reactant and then a suppressant."

Bigsy nodded. Elisa continued, "There's been a lot of speculation around forms of virus that can be airborne but also managed. Most people have heard of the Ebola virus in parts of Africa. It's been in movies as well, but actually even that virus really needs contact with living matter in order to spread. It's usually through the contamination of cuts or similar that create the spread and airborne spread is quite unusual because the virus can't survive."

"But what had been secretly happening in the labs was a series of defence-based investigations of ways to create airborne payloads of virus. This wasn't just being run by the Israelis, but also actually by a consortium of interests. The reason had been stated as defensive. To determine the virus effectiveness as a threat - and just as importantly, what techniques can be used as a way to stop it."

"...And the answer?", asked Clare, "How do you stop it?"

"That's the point," continued Elisa,

"There isn't a good answer. So far nature has been fairly kind to humanity on all of this."

"The really nasty viruses affecting humans won't travel by air alone. Ones that mutate heavily and are quite infectious - like influenza - will travel for a short time by air and exceptionally can kill but are generally less lethal.

"A combination of an airborne toxin with lethal characteristics has only happened a couple of times."

"Once was Anthrax - which was strictly a spore based biological weapon - and that had erratic, but deadly contagion characteristics. There were also a few US Chemical Corps attempts with fleas and mosquitoes as delivery mechanisms back in the 1950s."

"I see," said Clare, "The virus was actually hosted on something else, like the spore or the bug? So, it had some cells to keep it working whilst it travelled?"

"Exactly," said Elisa, "The spores and mosquitos were the delivery mechanism, and in each case, they were unpredictable to the extent that the whole process had to be stopped."

The Square

"Yes, and that Scottish Island with Anthrax is still off limits all these years later?" replied Clare.

"Let's say I don't think there's a line of people waiting to explore the island…" said Elisa.

"What evolved though from the various experiences, was a different delivery mechanism. It had to be fast acting over a small area and limited in terms of its long-term effect."

"They evolved a 'glass bomb' full of a compressed toxin protected by its surrounding enzyme. The virus had to be created just before use, because without its host it had a very short shelf life."

"The bomb could be broken and then spread toxicity at up to 50% for maybe a few square miles. Contagion would need to be within the first hour for it to be effective. Anyone affected would die but continue to be a host, creating a chain reaction in the area surrounding the release of the substance."

"A second timed capsule would release an antidote, which worked by breaking down the enzyme envelope that kept the virus protected as a way to limit the spread."
"It sounds awful, but entirely imaginable," said Clare.

"Is this work still taking place?" asked Bigsy.

"Not officially, actually it was Richard Nixon who ended the research in the late sixties."

"A long time ago. Surely there's not anything left?", queried Jake.

"Actually, there were a lot of people involved and they were effectively stopped from their main lines of research. Some of them may well have drifted off the rails since." added Elisa.

"Officially, there's been a virtual ban on this type of research since the nineteen-seventies, so that a sequel to atomic bombs was effectively stopped."

"Yeah, right", said Jake, "but how would anyone know?"

"Exactly," continued Elisa, "The Soviets and then the Iraqis continued with programmes. A Russian defector named their Biopreparat programme and then later its deputy director also defected to the USA."

"It's much harder to know what the Iraqis were doing, although they did admit to the U.N. that they had produced concentrated botulinum toxin during the first Persian Gulf War. The amount they produced was enough to wipe out the planet, except for the same distribution problem I mentioned with the viruses."

"So, what are we looking at here?", interrupted Clare. "It looks as if there's someone making a weapon which is some sort of virus. It can't survive for long in the air, but if it can be carried, then it could do a great deal of harm."

"Exactly," said Elisa, "It's the scenario we were simulating for years. A virus, effective airborne for short times and capable of being carried over other distances by a host such as an insect, without destroying its host in the process. It also needs to be stable and not modify itself, or else it becomes the new God of the planet."

They looked at one another.

"This is kind of doomsday," said Jake.

"Correct", added Elisa, "When we ran our scenarios, the only fully effective defence was to destroy it within the first hour, using the enzyme cracker. "

"Won't the people producing it have the same concerns about using it?", asked Clare.

"It's difficult to comment. Extremists, lunatics, mercenaries, criminals, people with nothing to lose. They may all take a different world view on such matters. We don't know what we are dealing with."

Elisa absently stirred the coffee cup and looked at the pattern on the surface.

"So how does it get used?" asked Bigsy. "It sounds almost too powerful to release?"

Chuck leaned forward. "There are three main scenarios. Sell it on, use it as threat or monetize it"

"I can understand the 'sell it on' scenario," said Clare, "but if it's such an unpredictable threat then who would actually use it?"

"That's where dealing with terrorists and criminals is so unpredictable," answered Chuck, "Sometimes ordinary logic doesn't work, plus there will be 'spin' from whoever holds the toxin. They will make it all sound safe and containable."

"Yes," continued Elisa, "the advanced work I was involved with in Israel before I was targeted was looking into the types of deterrent for this class of weapon. It was often a case of scientists trying to copy nature - something I thought was massively dangerous."

"Nowadays I look closely at news of new influenza strains or sudden crop devastation. That 2019-nCoV 'bat-bug' from Wuhan, China was a case in point. Did it display any of the characteristics of something engineered? Is it a cover-up because something has broken out of a lab somewhere?"

"What did you think?" asked Bigsy

"Well, it looks natural rather than machined. By using the Chinese virus as an example, we can see that nature is ingenious and has evolved the coronaviruses as large, enveloped, positive-sense, single-stranded RNA viruses that can infect both animals and humans. It's not been in the news, but there's four kinds, Alpha-, Beta-, Gamma-, and Delta-coronavirus. But all the CoVs that can infect humans belong to the first two types. The trick is to be able to store them somewhere and that's where the bat's DNA comes along as an ideal storage container. Let's remember that the bat has been around for 50 million years."

"Wow, plenty of time to get robust!" said Jake.

"Yes, don't get me started on spiders. They've been around for 380 million years," replied Elisa.

Chuck interrupted, "So I suppose what will have happened with the scientist development is the development of some kind of science-based storage container for the weaponised virus?"

"That's right," said Elisa, "Probably non organic, to keep the virus stable rather than see it further adapt,"

She continued, "We classify bioweapons by type. Toxins just kill everything in the radius. Herbicides like 'wheat blast' just take out the food stock in the fields. Neither of these are the type we are describing here"

"The one we are dealing with here is more sophisticated. It can be used selectively, targeted, do huge damage, but there can be an immunity vaccine. This one can be used to hold a planet to ransom."

"When I was at Ben Gurion University we developed and trialled something called the BioPen. It was originally a field diagnostic for many classes of chemo and bio attack - to help identify the type of weapon being used.

"The original pen used a technology called multiwells. They are microscopically small holes like mini test-tubes used to scan and detect the enzymes used in a biohazard. I think they are called microplates now, after some copyright fracas."

"The BioPen with these diagnostics could tell you what you were up against but it wasn't a cure."

"Then we worked out that if we knew the make-up of a viral hazard, we could use the same technology to deliver antibody enzymes. Basically, the BioPen could be modified to detect and immunise. It could be turned from a diagnostic into a field defence."

"So, as Chuck says, if someone wants to deploy the virus or to 'monetize' it then the modified BioPen becomes part of the process. It's either to provide immunity to the people deploying the virus, or to sell the antidote to the population being affected. The BioPen technology is what keeps it in balance."

"Is that like you see in the movies?" asked Clare. "The magic syringe that fixes everything?"

"I wish it were that simple," continued Elisa.

"We can't predict side effects. When it is viral, just like the flu bug or HIV, there's a type of modification which can occur. It's the natural mutation of the virus. Those that built this bioweapon know they have a tiger by the tail. It can be used as they intend it, or it could start to behave differently."

"The point with viruses is that they modify and unless you know enough about them you could spend years trying to figure a cure."

"That's why weapon-grade virus research was originally stopped. They could create the toxin, but no antidote. Except for the enzyme work linked to the pen. But the pen also relies upon knowing how the original virus had been constructed. Basically, you have a window to deploy and destroy."

Chuck interrupted "Exactly as Elisa describes it, there's a short time when you know what you are dealing with and can stop it."

Elisa nodded, "Yes, that's where mankind can't be as clever as nature. In a natural virus, it will self-modify but then stop once it has found a way to inhabit its host but keeo the host alive. The payoff for the virus is that it can persist for longer. A man-made virus won't have this check and balance. Just the BioPen to stop it."

"So, destruction at source is the only answer."

Elisa added, "Strictly there are still some other checks and balances:

One: Don't let the toxin get primed - hence the binary transport. Two: Use of the BioPen as an antidote. Three" The decay period of the toxin being short - like one hour. They are all equally effective safeguards against the latest neuro-toxin."

Chuck stirred his coffee for the fourth time.

"Look, I'll be accompanying Elisa back to her home, "She's not implicated in this at all but I wanted to get a sense of the situation from her. Elisa, I'm sure you'll be wanting to help us further?"

"Sure, Chuck, I just hope the scientists knew enough about what they were doing to build the virus in a way that keeps it stable. It's the best chance we have to destroy it."

A moment of silence and then Jake spoke.

"Er, so just what is it you want us to do again? This has got a lot wilder as each day passes."

He looked towards Chuck, who was working out what to say.

" Jake, it's the same deal. I just need you to run a diversion for me. I'll be meeting the main people involved with this and you'll be creating some separate theatre for the Secret Service to watch. When I get the information about the placement of the real toxin, I'll be bringing it in to be destroyed using the BioPen method that Elisa has described.

"The thing is, I'll want to know that every container has been neutralised so that we don't get back into the same situation. I don't want this to go through the normal channels because I'm afraid of the interceptions that could take place, whether it is US, Brit, Arab or Israeli, government or terrorist. Everyone's combined motive is to get to the material as a source of power and leverage. I just want it destroyed."

"There's a lot of American history around these neurotoxins actually," said Elisa.

"There were a couple of strains developed by the Americans at the time of the second Gulf War. They were called C1 and C2 (Yes, there is also a C3) and they were built to attempt to simulate the type of product that Saddam Hussain would be using.

Chuck said, "I remember that; gossip had it that they could even be used as a plant for WMD if things got really embarrassing. Morality prevailed and they were never shipped into Iraq, although the product was moved as far as Saudi Arabia, where they were stored on a USAF base near to Riyadh. I was still in the desert then, in the USA, and we had some contact with these so-called chemical and biological weapons."

Chuck added, "If I remember rightly, the Saudis were never informed. All comms related to this was at the highest and most secure level.

"Urban myth says the information leak was originally via a secret project called Room 641A. This was a splitter closet in San Francisco used for covert monitoring of signal intelligence.

"It's a fairly crude form of digital wiretap, to split the signal in half and send half to its proper destination and the rest to the NSA."

"Incredible," said Bigsy, "But I suppose the most blatant things can win out. Like those guys who built the trading intercepts for the flash trading on stock markets."

Elisa continued, "So a stream of discussion about C1 and C2 (also known as BK238) was initiated and tracked. There's another one, by the way, the well-known Novichok, which is categorised as A234."

"Ah yes, the Russian Wikipedia-loving assassins in Salisbury!" said Jake.

Elisa continued, "Right, and then the person monitoring the source used the ageing NIS (Narus Intercept Suite) to track down the calls and their purpose under the auspices of CALEA (Communications Intercept for Law Enforcement). It's old enough to have been something that Clinton's administration had originally set up for wiretapping but had extended to many matters of national security.

"In today's digital world, these all seem to be lightweight ways to provide the intelligence, so I'm assuming that there's better stuff available that hasn't leaked into the public domain.

"Anyway, on this occasion, the person had discovered what looked like a covert shipment of toxins to Saudi Arabia, without realising it was US DoD that was actioning the request.

"Ahah, said Bigsy, "So it is not just the US who use splitter programs and intercepts?"

"No, Bigsy, I don't think it would be a technical intercept. More likely to have been a human one this time," answered Elisa.

"The person had forwarded an alert under the PRISM surveillance program (SIGAD US-984XN) to the NSA but used his own grade level for the initial communication. The message had contained the phrase 'BK238' and its location in clear text.

"So a clear communication was intercepted? No wonder the US are sheepish about this!" said Bigsy.

"Yes, it was all that Al Aktar had needed to mobilise from within Saudi Arabia. A barracks was targeted with a conventional truck bomb as a diversion and a regular US Army vehicle with American mercenaries was dispatched to collect the cylinders from their safe store.

"The base had been pre-occupied with the bombing. The cylinder transit looked routine and the trucks had been able to drive from the base unchallenged. This all happened about three weeks ago."

"Yes," said Chuck, "But Al Aktar have done more than steal the neurotoxin." They have also stolen the smaller vials containing the antidote."

"Antidote?" asked Clare.

"Yes, the antidote can be used in a combat situation to neutralise the effect of the neurotoxin," answered Elisa, "It's not a perfect science, but it allows troops to be dropped into the kill-zone before the toxin has decayed."

"Ew," said Clare, "It's disgusting, like spraying people with fly killer and then going in to watch the effects."

"Yes, that is why we scientists were working to eradicate these kinds of terrible weapons," answered Elisa.

"Not to mention the small matter of them being illegal in just about every country," said Chuck, "You can see why a few superpowers are trying to make the whole situation go away."

"Yes, and why a few countries are now desperate to hide the fact that they have continued to work on this kind of weapon," added Clare.

Mesopotamian Heritage?

"Tell me about Al Aktar," asked Clare to Chuck, "You must know more about their origins?"

"Yes, it's deeper than Al Aktar, and goes back to the Iraqi mindset," replied Chuck, "The Al Aktar people had thoughts which went back much further than the war driven by George Bush.

"This group believed themselves to be part of the Iraqi Mesopotamian heritage, which was home to the Sumerian culture, dating back to 5000 BC. So, these should be smart people, with some of the first sciences and mathematics originating from the cradle of civilization.

"Wow, that's going back a long way," added Bigsy.

Chuck continued, "Later came Islam, with the prophet Mohammed's cousin and son-in-law moving his capital to Kufa "fi al-Iraq" when he became the fourth caliph.

The Square

"That's the start of the rise of Baghdad?" questioned Clare.

Chuck answered, "Yes, This led to Baghdad being the leading city of the Arab and Muslim world for five centuries but then, as early as the mid thirteenth century, Baghdad was devastated by the Mongols and later occupied by the Ottoman Turks.

"Such conflict would become a facet of this area, but the Ottoman Empire lasted right the way through until World War I when the Ottomans sided with Germany and were later driven from the area by the United Kingdom.

"For true Ottomans, this was only a short time to remember and British control of Mesopotamia with a United nations mandate created a lasting sense of colonial rule.

"Yes, that's the period I know more about," said Bigsy, "Iran under British rule,"

Chuck continued, "Occupation would be a better word. During the British occupation, the country was ruled by British administrators who used British armed forces to put down rebellions against the government. They selected the Hashemite king, Faisal, who had been forced out of Syria by the French, to be their client ruler.

"Between World War I and II, Iraq was granted independence, though the British retained military bases and transit rights for their forces in the country.

"King Ghazi of Iraq ruled as a figurehead after King Faisal died in 1932, while Iraq suffered from military coups until he died in 1939.

"This was all about the oil?" Asked Clare.

"Yes," said Chuck, "This led to the start of the fears of oil cutbacks and Iraq was again invaded by the United Kingdom in 1941, for fears that the government of Rashid Ali might cut oil supplies to Western nations and because of his strong leanings to Nazi Germany."

"Hmm, tricky," said Bigsy.

Chuck continued, "You could say that - A military occupation followed after the restoration of the Hashemite monarchy and this lasted until 1947. This reinstalled monarchy lasted until 1958, when it was once again overthrown through a coup d'état by the Iraqi Army, known as the 14 July Revolution."

"The coup brought Brigadier General Abdul Karim Qassim to power. He withdrew from the Baghdad Pact and established friendly relations with the Soviet Union but his government lasted only until 1963, when it was overthrown by Colonel Abdul Salam Arif."

"I think we must be nearly up to the Saddam Hussein era?" asked Clare.

Elisa nodded.

Chuck continued, "Yes, that's right. After Salam Arif's death his brother, Abdul Rahman Arif, assumed the presidency but was soon overthrown by the Arab Socialist Ba'ath Party. This movement gradually came under the control of Saddam Hussein al-Majid al Tikriti who acceded to the presidency and control of the Revolutionary Command Council (RCC), then Iraq's supreme executive body, in July 1979, killing off many of his opponents in the process."

"Saddam Hussein's rule lasted throughout the Iran-Iraq War (1980-1988) (in which the United States, Soviet Union, and France backed Saddam Hussein after 1982, at least in the open), a war that ended in stalemate.

"That backing of Hussein was because of oil?" asked Clare.

"Yes, strategic importance of the region," answered Chuck.

"In the late 1980s, Saddam Hussein's regime launched the so-called al-Anfal campaign (it means Spoils of War), which led to the disappearance of tens of thousands of Kurds (182,000 is the number given by Kurdish authorities for the year 1988 alone) in northern Iraq when the military razed thousands of villages, launched poison gas attacks and rounded up men, women and children before shooting them or burying them alive in mass graves."

"Note the poison gas, used this time," said Chuck, "It was instrumental in firing up new research by other countries."

"Yes, said Elisa, "Although there's a couple of aspects. There were some countries that had buried their research in deep cover. Other countries thought they would need some kind of R and D capacity for purely defensive measures."

Chuck continued, "Then, in 1990 Iraq invaded Kuwait resulting in the Gulf War and United Nations economic sanctions imposed at the urging of the U.S.

It left the U.S. In something of a quandary, having backed Hussein previously but now forced to turn against him.

The economic sanctions were designed to compel Saddam to dispose of weapons of mass destruction.

By that we mean the chemical and nerve agent weapons. Critics estimate that between 400,000 and 800,000 Iraqi children died as a result of the sanctions."

"The U.S. and the U.K. declared no-fly zones over Kurdish northern and Shiite southern Iraq to oversee the Kurds and southern Shiites."

"Iraq was invaded in March 2003 by a US-organised coalition with the stated reasons that Iraq had not abandoned its nuclear and chemical weapons development program according to United Nations resolutions."

"The justifications given for invasion included purported Iraqi government links to Al Qaeda, claims that Iraq had Weapons of Mass Destruction, the opportunity to remove an oppressive dictator from power, and the bringing of democracy to Iraq."

"That was all over the media, of course," said Clare, "But many people suspected that it was misleading."

"Yes," said Chuck, "A range of other possible motives include control over Iraqi oil fields, a desire to make amends for failing to overthrow Saddam during the Gulf war, revenge for Saddam's effort to assassinate former President George Bush, and creating a counterbalance to a nuclear-armed Iranian theocracy."

"There was even a theory that the war generated business for the U.S. based reconstruction contractors," added Bigsy.

Chuck nodded and then continued, "Subsequent post-invasion investigation did not uncover any evidence that the WMD programs were active; although some chemical shells were found that were left over from the Iran-Iraq War. Likewise, al-Qaeda had no presence in Iraq, where it had been suppressed by the secular Iraqi government, until after the invasion, when it exploited the insurgency to establish its organisation in the country.

"What about the rumours that America had WMDs stashed in Saudi Arabia and was going to plant them in Iraq?" asked Bigsy.

"Well, there's no evidence of that either," said Chuck, "Although these recent neuro-toxin findings make me begin to wonder."

Chuck continued, "The US established the Coalition Provisional Authority to govern Iraq. Government authority was transferred to an Iraqi Interim Government in 2004 and a permanent government was elected in January 2006.

"By 2006, over 140,000 Coalition troops remained in Iraq in order to assist the government in countering a Sunni-led insurgency, frequent terrorist attacks, and sectarian violence, which plagued the country.

"Then, in 2006, Foreign Policy Magazine named Iraq as the fourth most unstable nation in the world. I guess that is around when Al Aktar decided it was time to make their statements and to recover what they considered to be the state of Mesopotamia."

Chuck's involvement

"Chuck," asked Jake, "How come you're fighting the good fight alone on this one? You are usually tasked by a government."

"I have a history with this program," answered Chuck.

"I didn't realise it until Elisa's name came up again, but then I realised that the reason they had originally got me to protect Elisa was because of the biological work they were doing.

"Elisa isn't the only one, but the fact is, there's a set of scientists that have been kept on retention alongside the continuation of the bioweapon research. I hadn't realised it, but by helping Elisa I was also helping preserve this bioweapon threat. This is my way to settle things and clear up a mess."

"Are you acting independently?" asked Clare.

"Yes, well that is, I'm acting with you if you will support me."

"So not for a government or paymaster? And the end result is that the biohazard is destroyed?" asked Clare.

"Correct. This is one of my few completely self-run missions. And for the record, Chuck's Mission Guide 101 says 'Don't do self-run missions.'"

"That's why I need to keep it close. No-one will know any of you. Apart from the original 'Triangle' connection we have never been in contact."

"And we are not in danger?" added Bigsy.

"You should be okay. I will be in danger," said Chuck, "And the end result will be the removal of the threat. Completely."

"What are we supposed to do?" Asked Jake.

Chuck continued, "There will be a meeting. A sort of trade show where the owners of the weapon state their terms. It will be set up to look like an innocuous event. Just that the people there will be special."

"I'd like you to go along and to listen out for what is happening. It shouldn't be too difficult. They'll have some entertainment and that will make it easy for us to get some electronics in."

The Square

"We could provide the entertainment," said Clare, "we have the media contacts and I could pull some strings to get to the front of the line."

"It'd be with Christina Nott - who is a singer in any case. If you can help us find out how they intend to run this, then we can hook into the event management."

Chuck looked confused. Jake had never seen this before.

"It's not really my area," said Manners.

"No, but it is ours," answered Clare. "Let me get on to it."

"Do you need time to consider this?" asked Manners.

"We should, we need to know that Christina Nott is prepared to be in on it."

"Give us until tomorrow," said Clare, "Does Jake no how to contact you?"

"Put an entry on your website," said Chuck. Mention the word "Square" if it's a go or "Circle" if it's a no-go."

"I can do that," said Bigsy. "It'll be in the top article on the home page."

"By tomorrow, please," said Chuck, and then we will follow the process I've described to Jake."

"Basically, that I'll get a phone call with some instructions," answered Jake.

"Correct," said Chuck, "The coffees and pastries are on me." He stepped to the cash till, paid and waved to them, still seated.

They returned the gesture, slightly surprised at Chuck's sudden speedy exit.

"Man of action, even when eating cakes!" quipped Jake.

Bigsy grinned as he finished the last mouthful of Clare's chocolate dream cake.

"I told you this was large," said Bigsy.

"The cake? I got it for you," said Clare.

Jake turned to Clare and Bigsy, "Well, what do you think? This one seems crazier than ever."

"Yes, Chuck doesn't lead dull life, does he?" answered Bigsy.

"But he does have a twinkle in his eye when he asks us for help. I think he likes us," said Clare as she left the cafe.

"Oh, that's good to know, what could possibly go wrong?" answered Jake, walking briskly towards the bustling main road.

The Square

Jake hailed a taxi on the King's Road and the three of them climbed in.

"Altogether, that wasn't quite what I was expecting," said Jake.

"Chuck Manners doesn't lead a very normal life," added Clare.

"Are we going to do this thing or walk away?" asked Bigsy.

"Chuck hasn't mentioned it, but we do sort of owe him," said Jake.

"Two levels - one he helped us when we were in deep with that Lucien thing. Two, when the excess money came our way, he knew about it but has never mentioned it or hassled us."

"Jake's right," said Clare, " we do owe him, and he is saying that our role is peripheral."

"Yeah, I think Chuck will want to keep us out of any rumpus," said Bigsy, "He must know plenty of people who could help him with a fight."

They looked at one another. The taxi lurched over a speed bump and they all jumped slightly in the air.

"You know what," said Bigsy, "I have a great new story for the front of our web-site. About Squares…"

They nodded.

They were in.

Still in the taxi, Clare put in a call to Christina.

"Christina, I think I might have a gig for you, "she said, "Although it's not what it seems. Call me back."

Two minutes later Christina was returning the call. "I was on the tube. I just picked up your message."

"Not by phone. Let's meet" said Clare.

Clare met Christina to explain the proposition. They would need to provide facilities for an upcoming event.

Clare could pull strings so that they were asked to do the work and Christina would have to perform. It was all short notice, but it would be quite a coup for the organisers to get Christina Nott along.

Planning a gig

"Now I know what happens at a gig, I will be ready for it, next time--I will come in just a T-shirt and shorts and books, and fight my way to the front, like a quietly determined soldier, and then let the band take my head off.

I want to walk into rooms like that every night, with a sense of something happening."

— Caitlin Moran

Birmingham Mailbox District

Christina's meeting was scheduled to take place close to one of the Birmingham canals in the proximity of the area called the Mailbox. This up-and-coming area of Birmingham comprised some modern developments along the edge of the major canal infrastructure which cuts through the city.

The venue for the meeting was an attractive wine and champagne bar called Epernay and Christina had arrived early and decided to order a cocktail. Christina chose a comfortable seat close to the window which would make it easy for the people she was to meet to spot her when they entered the bar. In the opposite corner and close to the bar was a piano player who was dawdling out some jazzy tunes, languorously to the Sunday punters who were sitting drinking exotic cocktails and eating fancy canapes.

Christina had arrived alone for the meeting and had busied herself with some email on a notebook PC whilst she awaited the arrival of her contacts. In a slightly irritating way, she had been hit on by two men whilst she sat waiting, but they were good natured as she politely explained she was busy and waiting for someone. The piano player had noticed this too and looked across at one point as if to enquire whether Christina had wanted any help.

Eventually, the music contacts arrived and looked briefly around the bar before spotting Christina and making their way to where she was seated. There were three people, a tall slender woman with a knee-length leather coat, a flamboyantly dressed blonde haired guy with a dark suit jacket, purple shirt and red waistcoat and a dark haired rugged looking guy who looked as it he'd just come back from somewhere with unremitting sun.

They introduced themselves as Annalisa, Sacha and Douglas and made small talk about the weather in Birmingham and the accessibility of their current location.

"Whether you drive, take a taxi or bus, the only way to here for the last piece is on foot with a good view of everyone else who may be approaching the restaurant", said Sacha.

"This all sounds like a spy movie", smiled Christina, as she prepared to talk about the plans for the gig.

"Actually, Christina", stated Annalisa, "We are looking for some other help from you". Christina was intrigued with this and asked what they were talking about.

"The show we want you to do will be to a fairly large group", continued Annalisa. "and on this occasion, we will take care of all the ticketing. You'll still get a healthy split of the box-office. This is, in effect, a private concert".

"I thought it was a public concert?" queried Christina. "I'd expect to advertise and get some publicity as a result."

"We know it is a prestigious venue", replied Annalisa," We have a large group who wish to get together and your concert provides an ideal backdrop for their meeting. We can use the event to ensure that they all meet and transact a small amount of business with no one noticing that the group also has another interest."

Christina fiddled with her glass. She had only had one cocktail because she had wanted to keep a clear head for the meeting. Now she was glad she had, because the discussion had the chance to start going a little weird.

"What are you suggesting?", asked Christina. "I take it this is legal?"

Annalisa smiled. "Totally legal; we have the challenge to bring a large group together, allow them to swap some information and just to not create any ripples by being together. Your gig creates a perfect environment for this group of people to meet in a relaxed and entertaining setting.

"It's very simple", Sacha said, "We are creating an event in effect, a fully sold out concert. It will be in a prestige venue and the majority of the people there will have tickets.

"So, is there any risk to me or anything odd going on at this event?" asked Christina. "If it's drugs or anything then I'm not going to do it. I can walk away now, and it will be as if we have never met."

"There's nothing illegal or even slightly shady," said Annalisa. "We will, though, be using the event as a type of cover for a quite innocent meeting on another topic. I think you have already noticed that the fees are quite interesting."

Christina had noticed the fees for this event and that is what had attracted her to the meeting. It was significantly more than she had received for other appearances and could be the start of raising her profile. The deal included a well-above-average performance fee, a box split and even a bar split. Christina was beginning to wish that Clare had been able to attend.

Christina said, "I'm still interested. Let's talk about the date and the venue as well. I'll need to get my agent Clare to tidy up the details." This was definitely a situation where two heads would be better than one.

"Here's the plan", said Douglas, flipping open a small computer bag and extracting a couple of sheets of paper stapled together. "You'll find the details including the staging and the attendance numbers", he continued.

"We will give you an up-front payment, but if you still need to talk this over with your agent, then we will give you 24 hours to confirm your interest. We can't leave it longer than that and will need to find an alternative if you decline."

Christina was weighing this up. She liked the idea of the exclusive concert but had expected to be able to advertise and spread the word. If everyone was being invited to the session, then it may not get advertised or reviewed by the press, which was not ideal.

"Will there be press at the gig?" she asked, expecting that she already knew the answer.

"It's not very likely", answered Douglas, "We will want to keep the event very select - I think you consider it more like a large but private party. We'll also want to vet any production shots or crowd shots. Confidentiality is paramount."

"Okay", said Christina, "You'll get an answer from my agent tomorrow."

"And what is it likely to be?" asked Annalisa.

The Square

"It will probably be yes", replied Christina, already thinking about how to reach Clare quickly.

The three who had met Christina then started to make to leave the wine-bar. Sacha graciously paid the bill and the four of them left together. As Annalisa, Sacha and Douglas made to turn right from the entrance to the wine-bar, Christina walked in the opposite direction, over a short bridge and along a short piece of busy canal towpath back towards the city centre. She knew there was something unusual about what she was being asked, but the money being suggested for the gig seemed considerably better than other gigs she had performed and with her current unstable finances, the money would come in very useful.

A few minutes later, Christina was on the phone to Clare and recounting the story. Clare agreed it all sounded quite intriguing. "When do you get back to London?" she asked, "We can meet and decide what you want to do. I think you should do it, but maybe ensure that one of us is included in your back-up team. Even better if they can sing or play some tunes!"

Christina hailed a cab from the town centre back to the train station. She would be back in London in a couple of hours. It had been a strange day.

Clare had flipped off her mobile after the call from Christina and then called Jake.

"Hi, Jake, Christina's got the gig, but they don't want to advertise it. It sounds as if there is something else happening in the venue and that whoever is running it doesn't want to draw real attention to the situation. This could be something for us to have a look at!"

"Okay, " said Jake, "Team meeting at the 'Porter."

The Market Porter

Jake arrived first at the pub in London's Borough Market. He had grabbed a cab from outside the office and it had only taken about fifteen minutes to thread through the traffic to just south of the river.

Around him, there were many other Londoners standing, chatting animatedly and occasionally returning to the bar for more drinks. Jake wasn't a fan of the plastic beakers used when standing outside the pub, but still preferred this lively view to sitting inside with a proper glass but a less interesting vista.

Jake had also realised that he'd spent the whole day without eating anything and now noticed the sausage shop next door to the pub and was mulling over whether to spend the equivalent of a pint on a gourmet bap filled with the posh sausages on offer.

It was at this moment that Christina and Clare arrived together. Jake had known Clare longer than Christina and had originally met Christina when Clare used to want to support Christina at various small gigs sprinkled around London. Originally Christina had been a well-travelled singer with an acoustic guitar but had later adapted to a more commercial dance style of music, which had also been the basis of her modestly successful CDs and iTunes track downloads.

Christina was also adept at creating appearances which could range from stunningly eye-catching to being able to blend into the scenery to avoid attracting attention. Today, Christina was out with her friend Clare and the two of them were dressed to a matching level and would certainly turn heads but not attract the wrong kind of attention whilst they walked through the market.

"Would you like a drink?", asked Jake, "or shall we find somewhere we can sit down?" The venue was a great place to wait for one another but wasn't the best location for a private conversation about what had been happening. "Let's go around the corner," suggested Clare. There was a nearby exit from the market area, and this led onto a busy main road. Just around the corner was a doorway and some stairs leading down into a subterranean wine bar.

"This will do fine," said Christina. "It's a quiet enough place for me to be able to tell you what has happened and ask for your advice".

They traversed the stairs into the wine bar. It looked as if it had been constructed in a cellar and there was a neat looking bar area with a couple of people standing waiting to serve them. "Shall we have a bottle?" asked Clare. The others both nodded and Clare requested a bottle of white wine and three glasses. They selected a table and Jake started to pour the wine.

"Tell all," said Jake to Christina, "Just what are you getting yourself into?"

Christina explained about the possibility of the gig, the meeting with the Italians, and the slightly strange way that the venue and conditions had been specified.

"Perhaps it's the Mafia!" said Jake. There was a pause and then he could see that his joke was slightly backfiring. "Er, I'm joking, you know."

Christina looked at Clare and they both smiled. Jake realised he had just been out-manoeuvred.

"I forgot", said Jake, "When you two are together, I don't stand a chance if I want to 'wind you both up'."

"Right," said Clare laughing, "You know when you are outclassed!"

Christina also smiled. "I did, initially start to wonder things like that myself", she admitted.

"The original arrangements for us to meet were straightforward enough, and the plan was for Clare to also be at the meeting. It was only a last-minute thing that meant I had to go alone. I'm sure my imagination has just been working overtime."

Jake agreed. Christina had been asked to perform a music concert at an attractive venue. The guests were to be personally invited by the Italian organisers and there would not be any public admission. Disappointed, Jake didn't think there was anything suspicious after all.

"So where is the gig and how much do you get?" he asked as a prelude to changing the subject. Christina's reply made him change his mind.

"What?" he exclaimed, "That is a lot of money for a private show and to such a large group, too. They must really like you a lot!"

"Precisely", replied Christina, "Now do you see my point!"

Jake, Christina and Clare had continued to work their way through the bottle of wine.

Clare and Christina had pretty much decided to accept the deal with Annalisa and the Italians, and Clare was to call them first thing in the morning. If needed, Clare would dispatch paperwork and contracts for the gig by Christina.

The Square

The three of them could not decide if there was really something suspicious about the requested performance. The money on offer for Christina to perform was probably three times as much as Christina's wildest expectation to the point where Christina and Clare somehow wondered if the whole thing had been a hoax.

Jake knew, however, from his journalism work that there were plenty of examples of people from the pop industry being offered everything from advanced copies of new materials, through to petty theft by musicians of tunes and riffs to unusual methods to hype a record or group to the top of the charts. He supposed that the angle on Christina was something like this, although he couldn't quite work out how the scam was operating.

"Don't sign anything without reading it properly first," he offered as rather obvious advice.

Christina and Clare stifled grins, both aware that there was still something unusual about the gig planned for Birmingham.

Ed Adams

Fake News

"You are fake news."

— Donald J. Trump

The Square

Carson's meetings

Colonel Carson was being given an ultimatum. He wanted to stay in his senior role and was now being told that the situation was a matter of Homeland Security. Carson was loyal, so it was inconceivable that he would not follow the order, or in this case the request.

"We need to top and tail the travel arrangement. Terrorists can gain an upper hand in the United States if we don't do something about it. Our citizens are becoming disaffected with the ever-increasing level of threats to the United States. We are now squeezing the various air travel trips because of the heightened security, plus eco-concerns.

Carson had been involved with some tough and some covert situations, but he wondered here what he was being asked to do,

"We want you to help us turn the opinion around," continued another suited man. He had not seen him before and considered that it was probably a civilian advisor to the government.

"What are you asking?" quizzed Carson.

"We need to create a change of focus," continued the advisor. "It involves moving the emphasis from North America. We are seen by most of the middle east as the enemy and there is little sympathy for anything we do to try to support or improve anything in any of the middle eastern counties.

" We need the next wave of terror attacks to be elsewhere; somewhere in Europe is the preferred location. This will give the USA a chance to clear its portfolio and for any next round of counter measures to be led from another base. America First, remember.

"The United States is having too many problems at the moment. Most of our electorate want our people back home, not stuck in a desert somewhere. At home there's major paranoia associated with possible further terrorist attacks and there is a real risk that another big thing could happen.

"Even when The White House opens its mouth or tweets something, there's a risk of ripples from around the globe. We are getting too much of the wrong kind of attention."

"That's why we need for something bad, originated from an identifiable hot-spot, but deployed in say London or Paris. There will be a forced acceleration of their involvement in retaliation and the focus will inevitably shift to those areas where the most damage had occurred."

Carson was taken aback. He'd been asked to do some pretty covert missions in the past, but usually involving unstable regimes that just needed small push to tip them into some form of junta or major change. This was different; he was being asked to devise a way to shift terrorist activity away from the United States by creating activities in another country. He was also being, in effect, asked to incite a declaration of war from those other countries against the Middle East. This was like starting a World War Three.

"I'm not sure about this," ventured Carson, "I've had to do some pretty big things in my time, but this is huge".

"We thought that might be your reaction," said the suited advisor. "We have worked out the main plan and let me assure you that your part in this will be strongly acknowledged. I don't mean gallantry medals or anything that leads back to you in a dangerous way, but let's just say we have a very large budget for this assignment and its leader will be rewarded in a way that means they won't need employment after this and can live very well indeed.

Carson considered. If he said no, but already knew what this was about, then he would be in some danger anyway. If he said yes, he would need to take his chances during the mission and needed to find a way to disappear with whatever was on offer at the end of the mission.

"Count me in," he said decisively, "But you will need to explain to me in more detail what we are supposed to do."

The Advisor introduced himself more fully, "I am Deputy chief of staff Brendan Cullane, advisor to the US Armed Forces and to the President. There are several people like me, who operate in a special capacity in times of extreme difficulty. We are always around but the nature of our office is kept rather quiet."

Carson was aware of this from a similar experience on a more minor scale when he had been asked to do something in Sudan a few years ago. He had been involved with an operation which required a silent entry and exit from the country along with the extraction of one key individual. The circumstances were that the whole mission had to be accomplished without any media or military attention. He'd worked with a small team of free-lancers for that and the whole mission had run very smoothly.

He had been given a briefing by the advisor on that occasion and was somewhat amazed at the diplomatic and clandestine tricks which were smoothly pulled in order to make the whole operation successful.

This would be another situation like Sudan, only on a much larger scale and potentially disadvantaging some of the European Superpowers. He was still somewhat shocked by this but knew that total commitment to the plan was his only real option.

"So, explain the mission," asked Carson.

Cullane continued, "We intend to divert attention from the USA as a consequence of a major terrorist attack in mainland Europe. Rest assured that the terrorists are planning to do this anyway. The effect will be to galvanise the countries affected to strong and decisive action to put down the attackers and to take control of the country harbouring the terrorists.

"The impact on the USA will be to deflect much of the current attention away. Both in terms of terrorism and also in terms of our contribution to the war efforts in the Middle East.

"Our current action is becoming unpopular with the citizen electorate and also our military support is extremely expensive, far beyond our original estimates. The other economic support industries are still working well, so a reduction in our level of arms will help redress the overall balance well.

"If the British and Germans take a stronger interest in the region, then they would help this economic re-balance.

"Your role is to ensure that a plot already in progress is deflected from US shores. We have picked up intelligence that the Al Aktar organisation have been busy recently and have gained access to some nerve agent which originated from Israeli testing.

"Al Aktar are stealing the nerve agent and are intending to use it in some attacks dependent upon the highest bidder.

"There will be some kind of decoy attack and we believe this will be some sort of rocket attack into an airport or similar, and that this will create a diversion whilst their main attack was run.

"We can ensure that the resultant news coverage is suitably pointed. And that it will deflect away from the United States.

"What?" asked Carson, "Manipulation? Of the News?"

"We want you to ensure that Al Aktar are discouraged from thoughts of using this in any of the Homeland territories. If anything is going to happen it needs to be elsewhere. We think they will also have a decoy operation. Both need to be managed.

"But what about the nerve gas? Won't it be so lethal that it breaks all of the conventions of war?", asked Carson.

"Yes, the nerve gas is very strong, but there are some aspects of the way it will be deployed which keep us in control.

"We don't know why they are doing this at the moment. It could be ideology, but it seems to be being driven by some other financing, which we've not managed to unscramble. This looks like a case of giving a weapon to someone prepared to use it indiscriminately - except they can't afford it, but someone else is paying the bills."

"Shouldn't we just alert everyone and try to stop it?

"Yes, we could do that, but the likelihood is that the terrorists would simply turn attention back to the United States. At the moment, we have a confidence that we can run faster than anyone else from the pursuing wild animal.

Carson nodded. He knew the old story with the punchline 'I just have to be faster than you' when escaping from a tiger.

"Who else knows about this?" Asked Carson.

"Just us - and the President," answered Cullane.

Weight throwing

Robert Alton was back at his SI6 office. Dorothy came through on the phone, "There's a US Colonel on the phone for you. A Colonel Carson."

Alton grimaced, "Thank you Dorothy, you'd better put him through," Alton knew that Dwight Carson was one to throw his weight around and quite capable of small-time blackmail and threats to get his own way.

"Dwight, to what do I owe this pleasure?" he began.
"Hello Robert, I think you might be in some kind of trouble at the moment. We are aware of an explosion near Cairo. Word has it that some of your people were involved."

"What is that to which you are referring?" asked Alton.

"Don't play dumb with me, we both know you had Karen Martin along for a rendezvous... That she was managing the Egyptian situation on the ground, from Cairo... That she commissioned a stringer to go out to exchange data with the truck driver. I'm keeping it out of the media here, as we speak."

"You know that we'll have to deny it all?" answered Alton, "It's easier now with so much Fake News around."

"It's luck then that we've got a photograph of Karen waiting at the cafe, for her stringer, and then another one of him walking past the spot, just before she was murdered. James, I think that was his name."

Alton looked dismayed, "Even if what you say was true, why would you be calling me about it now? Why not two days ago?"

"Two days ago, we didn't need anything. Now we want something from you. Something that I guarantee will make this go away."

"Go on," said Alton.

"We know that James has made contact with an American. We think the contact is ex-military. We just need a name. We have, shall we say, some interest in him and his association with James."

Alton was thinking quickly. Now he'd met Chuck Manners and seen that he was a professional and something of a slippery character. He decided that Chuck could handle himself.

"And if I could provide this information?"

"Then we'll lose the evidence about your UK involvement in the recent helicopter crash and truck destruction."

"I want something else," asked Alton, "The name of your parallel operative. - An eye for an eye, after all." He wanted to see if he could push Carson, to find out how desperate he was.

"So, we have a deal?" asked Carson.

"If you provide us with the information. It also gives me something to show as collateral from the trade." Alton smiled. Carson was desperate.

Carson paused, "Okay. We'll forgo escrow protocol, you give me the name now, and I'll give you the name in return."

Alton thought - Carson is really desperate.

Alton said, "Colonel Chuck Manners."

Carson paused again, Alton could hear some noise in the background.

"And your field agent was?"

"A stringer also - US citizen, Steve Ruben."

Alton was aware that Carson had just thrown the US stringer to the wolves. He hoped that he had not done the same for Chuck Manners.

"Okay, thank you for that, I'll see you at the next NATO session, probably," said Carson, "Over and Out"

Alton felt suitably trampled over by Carson. He was the proverbial bull in a china shop and simply didn't care how he obtained his information. In a few minutes Alton had been threatened, and then seen a US asset thrown away to get what Carson wanted.

Tracker lock

Carson's mood escalated when he heard the news from Alton. That Colonel Chuck Manners was deployed alongside the UK stringer "James" raised the game.

Carson was aware of Manners from varied black-ops dotted around the world. He had a staggering success rate and yet he seemed able to disappear from view between operations.

Now he alerted his own operations centre. They were to track James, whose cell-phone ID they had already captured and Chuck Manners, whose cell-phone could be tracked back via his stay in Cairo. They needed his hotel room and then they would have a fix on the unique identifier of the American-issue cell phone, which legally had to carry its own tracking device.

Carson was familiar enough with the Fourth Amendment to know that he could break it to find Manners and used the US5519760A Cellular network-based location system as the basis for a tracker alert.

From this, his operations centre could see that Chuck had been close to James in Egypt, even in the same sector of desert as the truck. They had then split up and travelled separately to New York. That James had then travelled to Nice and Cannes in France, and that Chuck had followed a day or so later.

They were currently co-located in Cannes, France.

-.-. . .-.. .-.. - .-. .- -.-. -.- / .. ... / .-. . .- .-..

Chuck picked up his cell phone.

"Hi Chuck, it's Robert Alton,"

"Hi Robert, this is unexpected?"

"Yes, the worst news I'm afraid. A Colonel Carson in the US DoD has requested your name and we've had to supply it. I guess he will be looking out for you now. Please consider this a heads up."

Chuck looked around, "How long ago?" he asked.

"Less than an hour, but I expect you are being tracked."

"Okay," said Chuck, he looked at his phone, "I'll do a reverse lookup to see who is tracking me, and thanks for letting me know. I'll go dark now. Expect a text with my new phone."

Chuck looked at his phone, he accessed an App called Celltrack. He pressed a special key combination and sure enough it revealed that there was a tracker lock on the phone. He wrote down the codes for it. Then he ejected the SIMM.

He knew that was not enough now that the trackers had got his phone's device identity.

He walked outside to the busy street. A builder's truck from Newcastle-Upon-Tyne was stuck in the traffic. He gently tipped the still switched on phone onto the truck's open rear platform.

"Bye bye," he said, "Happy trails."

Bad America

Major Garcia Ramirez reported to Colonel Dwight Carson in the Special Operations Unit, based in the Pentagon.

Ramirez himself was a career military person and had distinguished himself in the first Gulf war. He was now involved in senior and special work, and Carson was his normal direct reporting officer.

Colonel Carson operated in a shadow world. He was involved with politics to a greater degree than anyone else that Ramirez knew, but it had normally served his department well, because it was usually easy to get funding for new projects or special operations. In that respect, Carson took care of his team.

But Ramirez wondered what else there was to know about Carson. He seemed to be out of the office a lot, had various secret high-powered meetings and treated a lot of information on a strict need to know basis.

This created an image of mystique around Carson and Ramirez was one of the people who sometimes wondered what Carson's full agenda entailed.

The reality was very complex. Carson had direct access to the President of the United States and access into the major areas of the CIA, FBI and NSA. Carson was also well connected and senior in military terms and so could get his own way on many matters.

As a result, they often sought his opinion from high levels within the US government and Ramirez suspected that some of this opinion giving was off the record.

Examples included opinions about the second gulf war, including some kind of direct involvement in the discussions about the Weapons of Mass Destruction. But Ramirez also knew that Carson had been operating long before the Iraq war started officially.

Carson had been involved in the planning of a series of air raids in an air corridor which started several months before the formal war started. The plans driven covertly by the Americans were to start to destroy certain kinds of border environments and logistic support points well before a war really kicked off. This gave the US military some early advantages because they both knew some terrain but as importantly had already destroyed most of the military hardware used by the Iraqis.

The Square

Ramirez had been sent into the area at this time, into Saudi Arabia, to act as a nearby observer and to provide logistical support if required during the period that the bombings were intensifying. The most difficult press reports to suppress at the time were the Al Jazeera television reports. This was interesting to Ramirez, because although the main language of the television station was Arabic, there were an increasing number of English language reports being produced which described in some detail the missions which were underway.

Ramirez had been situated in Saudi Arabia's capital city of Riyadh for the majority of his time in the country. He had been posing as a civilian worker and was based at a Sheraton Hotel not far from the downtown area. It was a short drive to the military camps, but he preferred to stay close to the hotel and to have people visit him, suitably dressed down and definitely not in uniform.

Ramirez had found the operation to be fairly predictable, involving some spin of the things that were taking place and some reasonable bribes to be placed to prevent certain stories from surfacing. During this time, Ramirez had seen Carson at work close hand for the first time. It was obvious that he knew his way around the people, but also the customs and what could and could not be done and said.

And at present, it was obvious to Ramirez that Carson was involved in some special agendas. Ramirez tried to speculate what Carson knew or was doing, but it was not so very obvious. Carson had been to several meetings with Chiefs of Staff and direct advisors to the President. It was obvious that there was something happening, but Ramirez had no idea what it might be.

Brief Ramirez

Major Garcia Ramirez was sitting with Colonel Dwight Carson.

"This situation…There's something wrong with it isn't there?" asked Ramirez.

"Yes, I'm stuck between a rock and a hard place," answered Carson.

"If you are, does that mean I am as well?" asked Ramirez.

"Let's just say the President is involved."

"You'd better explain."

"You know that black-ops chopper that was downed in Egypt?"

Ramirez nodded.

"It was Israeli, operating across the Border."

"That's like an act of war, isn't it?" asked Ramirez.

"Unless it has been condoned, and I suspect the US put on pressure to let it take place."

"What was it doing, blowing up some road traffic or something, wasn't it?" asked Ramirez.

"Correct," said Carson, "In fact, it was blowing up a missile transport."

"That's why the reported explosion was so large?" asked Ramirez.

"Not exactly; the truck was transporting something else. Not missiles. Neurotoxins."

"What? They are outlawed. Had the Egyptians been making them? We are in WMD territory here."

"No, the toxins were originally manufactured in the USA. Then they were shipped to Israel for testing."

"Something went wrong during the tests and they had to close the lab."

"Fatalities, or what?"

"Yes, everyone. Everyone in the lab was killed. The neurotoxin has around a one-hour life, unless re-hosted."

"So, what was it doing on a truck?"

"We'd done a deal with the UK. To ship it to Porton Down for destruction. Except for a very small amount which would be held in their sample bank."

"I see, instead of holding the dangerous materials in Nevada, we're outsourcing it now. Very smart."

"Yes, the Brits think it is a sweet arrangement."

"What were they doing in Egypt?"

"The route was road and sea. Egypt, Libya, Tunisia, Algeria, Spain, Santander and then sea to the UK. It was intended to be low profile, compared with going across the whole of mainland Europe."

"Libya though? Surely that is a hornets' nest?"

"Yes, but since the UN 'unity' Government, there's a hint of American control. And it should have been one Arab-plated truck, looking like an oil truck."

"But the truck didn't make it?"

"No, the Israeli helicopter blew it up, with extra powerful munitions to destroy the toxins. Then the chopper was downed as well. We think that was by an American freelancer - Colonel Chuck Manners."

"But doesn't that mean the mission is finished?" asked Ramirez.

"Ordinarily, yes, but on this occasion there's something else. A second truck. Another set of neurotoxin warheads."

"Where are they now?"

"No-one knows. The trackers have been demobilised and we don't know who is controlling the operation."

"Who knows about this?"

"Almost no-one. A few advisors and the President. I doubt if the truck drivers even know what they are carrying."

Ed Adams

Unstoppable

I'm unstoppable
I'm a Porsche with no brakes
I'm invincible
Yeah, I win every single game

I'm so powerful
I don't need batteries to play
I'm so confident, yeah, I'm unstoppable today
Unstoppable today, unstoppable today

Sia Furler

Al Aktar

Al Aktar was a trading company shell with Iraqi-based owners. They had never claimed their Iraqi origins in the UK and instead pretended to be Lebanese.

Their view was that Lebanese were generally accepted to the point that Lebanese restaurants and food were a very acceptable part of British culture, whereas Iraqi connotations immediately created ripples leading towards the George Bush war and even echoes back to the events of September 11.

The headquarters of Al Aktar Trading was a small depot in a factory estate near to the A4 main road to London. It was in an area sandwiched between railway tracks and arches.

Nearby, an elevated section of the M4 motorway leading between London and the London Heathrow Airport created continuous noise. The entrance to the trading estate advertised van rental and shot blasting, along with a mobile phone number. This was a fairly rough part of town.

The environment was a low-rise series of buildings where double-glazing depots, carpet warehouses and a small company who installed car alarms were grouped together. There was a steady traffic of cars, vans and small trucks, which was a combination of private customers and low-end tradesman.

This was the area where the middle eastern traders were able to run a bland-looking business in a way which pretty much escaped detection.

There was always some bustle from the premises and occasionally people engaged in prayers at certain key times of the Islamic day. But the people kept themselves to themselves. They wore mainly simple western clothes, although sometimes there would be visitors in more overt Arabic clothing. But the location and the type of visitors did not seem unusual or special.

The reality was very different, because this trading company held a cell of a terrorist unit with plans to destroy key parts of the London infrastructure.

"We can control via asymmetric warfare", explained Ali Al Mansour.

"The power we bring can crush opposition and make strong our view."

In the corner sat another western-looking man, in his late forties, but tanned and fit, looking like a soldier or ex-soldier and certainly someone who could handle himself.

"Correct," he commented, "We have some extensive plans for the next two weeks". He looked around the room meaningfully, "Is everyone clear that they want to help?".

Ali Al Mansour repeated the question in Arabic and there were a few yelps of support from those in the room. Al Aktar was forming its army of destruction and had the first block of recruits ready for action.

"Let's go through the plan", continued Al Mansour.

"Not now", responded the European, looking down to the floor, "When we have a clearer plan, I will want to brief people in groups. I don't want everyone to know all aspects in case someone is captured."

Al Mansour nodded his agreement. "Then tonight we send people away, and then meet again in smaller groups, maybe at the mosques."

The European nodded again and walked towards the door. As he did so, a black car pulled up outside the office. He stepped into the back seat and waved the car away.

-... . .-- .- .-. .

The Square

Al Aktar had created their base camp in Egypt. It was far enough from Cairo to be inaccessible to casual travellers, yet close enough to benefit from the transport infrastructure. It was also outside of the usual zone of spy planes and satellite surveillance which would attract attention in any of the "-istans".

The White Desert is a large area of remote desert yet the four strategic oases of Bahariya, Farafra, Dakhla and Kharga provided water, accommodation and ready transport together with a traffic of tourists which provided good cover for the terrorist cells as they moved people into and out of their training and briefing centres.

Khalid Al Sharif was the head of the cell and had run several briefings to recent groups about the plans for ways to destabilise the western economy.

To achieve this, they needed significant weapons, and had decided to infiltrate the DoD to achieve this. They would need to know where significant weapons were stored and when they were due to be transported.

A contact high in the US military had been identified who could be leveraged to provide the basic information. The contact had asked for money, both for himself and to pay another person, from the UK security services.

Al Attar's plan was to hit two major financial centres in Europe, in a way that would create mass outward movements of money. This would have a devastating effect upon the Western economy of Europe, as money was moved to other parts of the world.

There would be a combination of civilian casualty from the acts of terrorism, but there would also be a great levelling of the conditions between Europe and the Middle East as a consequence of the outflow of money and the collapse of companies.

The level of this required major impacts in the areas to be affected, and in London there were features such as the transit system which could help the effective spread of a chemical agent.

In Frankfurt it was slightly harder because there was no equivalent of the London Underground, but the major intention was to get two major exclusion zones created for the city centres of London and Frankfurt. The plan required careful co-ordination such that the two planned attacks would happen within a short time of one another.

Al Aktar was using the desert base as a briefing and training centre for the people to be involved in the attacks and because the training camp was close to a tourist route through the desert it had the advantage of ease of access without undue suspicion.

There were several companies which conducted tours in the area, and Al Aktar had created its own company for the same purpose, with the exception that guests were all part of the terror cells. It was a bold plan but worked well and created little suspicion.

Another camp in Pakistan was used for firearms and general fitness training and it was only the elite who passed through into the Cairo desert base on their way to full deployment.

Khalid Al Sharif was in a meeting with several of the key operatives. "Most people will not know the full plan", he said," You are a few privileged to know what we plan to do. We will take the nerve agents and deploy them in two city centres. We will also create diversions at nearby major airports as a way to distract large amounts of military from our primary purpose."

"There will be a couple of random attacks on civilian planes as the start of the plan. We will detonate planes on the ground. This is symbolic and will create huge flows of police and emergency services to the respective airports. Whilst this occurs, we will launch our primary attacks in the two major city centres. This will involve the release of nerve agents, simultaneously from several key locations in each city centre. The diversion of the airport attacks will create confusion which allows our primary purpose to be achieved."

"There are a lot of questions," said one of the people being briefed.

He was a 25-year-old, with a dark beard and wore desert clothing and dark glasses.

"How do we attack the airport and what happens when we release the nerve gas?"

"First there will be an attack on airports using Saudi Air Force Missiles which we have acquired via a series of contacts.

"We are incorporating them into the design of a couple of trucks for shipment to the respective countries

"The nerve agent is very compact and can be handheld by our followers up to the moment of deployment. They will be martyrs as a consequence of freeing the chemicals into the air. The chemical agent is of a power that each cylinder will affect 50,000 people. Once in the system, such as the railway system, it will have devastating reach."

The group receiving the briefing talked briefly amongst themselves. "Will we be martyrs as part of this?", one of them asked. "No, your job is to find the believers who will take the chemical to the places where it needs to be deployed. You will ensure that trusted men carry forward this mission", replied Khalid Al Sharif.

"And how will the airport part be handled?" asked another.

"We have already selected a driver to take the payload across Europe and we have two locations where the commissioning can take place. We have been planning this for a long time, we are well bankrolled and have access to the necessary people," continued Khalid Al Sharif.

Ed Adams

Unstable

Back at the Al Akram industrial site in London, Mehdi Akram was shaking his head.

"Those delivery drivers Alan and Dave were duped by UK government forces. The last BioPen vial was handed over to the UK instead of to us."

"Do you want us to fix them?" asked Ghali Yessim.

Mahdi Akram replied, "Ordinarily I would say yes, but I don't want to draw any unnecessary attention to ourselves. We should put the missing vial down to a cost of war and let the two drivers go. Let's face it, they have only made half their money and we have nearly all of the BioPen vials."

The BioPens each had a small glass window at the top, which had started a clear green colour. On a few of the containers it was beginning to change to a yellow/green colour.

"It is the start of the decay process for the BioPen content, said Mehdi Akram, "Normally these pens should last for several years. It can only mean that the handling has been compromised. "

Ghali Yessim asked, "Does that affect their usefulness?"

"There's a significant safety margin built into the warning display. They should be good for several months beyond their decay point."

"Even so, it will be harder to shift them if they look defective," said Firas Belhassan, "Maybe I can rig the warning lights?" Said Firas Belhassan, "Let me have a try."

He opened it cautiously.

Ghali said, "Just don't be pressing the release mechanism. The pen should only be used against the neurotoxin. In concentration it is also virulent."

Firas gingerly did things to the BioPen vial and made the light reset to green, "See. I can short the detection circuit. Let's do it on the rest,"

He worked his way through the first box. Successfully. Then he move along to the second box, about to start the same process again.

"Ach!" he announced, "I've tripped the mechanism on this one." It had accidentally released some of the antidote onto his skin.

He wiped it off with his hand and continued and he continued the process with the second box of BioPens. As he finished, he looked back towards his hand. A large blister was forming where the antidote had struck. He could see it was tracing the arteries in his arm.

Mehdi Akram looked over. "Firas Belhassan, my friend, I think you have been infected. Infected with the antidote. Without anything to work against, I fear it is unstoppable.

Truck Two

Major Garcia Ramirez was thinking about Truck Two. For the Israelis to have tracked the first truck they must have known its whereabouts. The strike was cleanly executed and precise.

It implied that there was either excellent intelligence about the trucks' movements, or more likely that there was a tracker of some kind on the vehicle.

If so, then who would place it there.

The Americans? Unlikely, or he'd already know about the device.

The British? Possibly; they were taking control of the toxin at its destination.

The Egyptians? Unlikely, and they would also be unable to keep the information secure.

The Israelis? They would need the transmitter to be able to locate the truck from the helicopter.

In all probability, the British had supplied the Israelis with the tracker code.

Ramirez would need to be onto his contacts in both UK and Israel. They would certainly deny it, but he had something that he thought they would need. His silence over the first mission.

He put through a call to London. He could be blatant, it would be a shorter route to the people who knew anything.

Dorothy entered Robert Alford's office. "I've a Major Ramirez on the phone for you," she said, "It seems to be about something that happened in Cairo. It's come through on a diplomatic line."

"You'd best put him through," answered Robert Alton.

"Robert Alton?" queried Ramirez, "I think we need to talk."

"On what matter?" asked Alton.

"The stealth Israeli helicopter for which the Brits gave a precision tracker code and which blew up a tanker in transit across the desert," bluffed Ramirez, "I have pictures," he lied.

"Just supposing that were true, why take so long to come through to us?" asked Alton unrattled, "I assume you want something?"

"Correct," said Ramirez, "You will know that there are two trucks on the loose. One has been found and dealt with, the other one is still out there."

"And why would I be interested in that?" asked Alton.

"You'd want to know that the neurotoxin was safe on its transit from Tel-Aviv to Porton Down," bluffed Ramirez.

"Ah, yes, I see what you are speculating," said Alton, "I don't suppose it has occurred to you that the original munition was developed in the United States? At the Edgewood Chemical Biological Center."

Ramirez was taken aback. He had heard of Edgewood, in Maryland, but didn't know it was capable of nerve agent development. Maybe Alton was also bluffing?

"Full disclosure?" asked Alton.

"Okay," said Ramirez.

"What you said has a semblance of truth about it," answered Alton.

"You did provide the codes to the Israelis?" asked Ramirez.

"Let's understand how we got to this position. America developed the neurotoxin - against international agreements, and then shipped some of it to the Saudi desert, where you put it into storage at an Air Force base. Then, you sent some more to Tel-Aviv, for further refinement. The Tel-Aviv samples went rogue and wiped out a lab. You asked for the toxin to be destroyed, as well as for a small sample to be kept, and started the movement towards Porton Down, UK."

"That's consistent with what I know," bluffed Ramirez.

"Did you know that Al Aktar found out about the shipment and were planning to intercept and steal it?" asked Alford.

"They have already stolen the BioPens which contain an antidote for the nerve agent."

"If they get the container with the second batch, they will have a complete neurotoxin kit. Except for one thing. They also need to code to arm the neurotoxin."

Ramirez said, "You'll have to explain that last part to me?"

"Well the neurotoxin can't be shipped in a primed state. Instead there's a two-part container, with the bulk of the reactant in one compartment, but a smaller internal container which has to be digitally activated by a code."

"Okay," said Ramirez, "I'll level with you. We are only interested in the truck at the moment. The one with the containers. We want to destroy it and the containers of nerve gas. Much like the Israelis did with the first truck."

"Yes, well that's the challenge," said Alton, "The trackers have gone dark."

"Since when?"

"Since about two hours after the first truck was destroyed."

"Okay, so you must know the other truck's approximate route?"

"Yes, it was heading across mainland Europe. It was in Turkey when we last had access."

"I'll guess the route then," said Ramirez, "Ankara, Istanbul, Sofia, Belgrade, Vienna, Frankfurt, Cologne, Brussels, Calais."

"How can you know that?" asked Alton.

"Sat-Nav," replied Ramirez, "Think about it, a truck driver wants to take the shortest or speediest route to the UK. He'll dial it up on Google or Sat-Nav. It's effective too, because we'd need a roadblock to stop it, rather than a missile strike on those busy roads."

Alton paused, Ramirez had made a good point.

"But we don't know where the truck is, nor do we have its tracker co-ordinates."

"Agreed, but we know when it stopped and where. The NSA has a great little phone signal tracker RTLS - Real Time Locating System - We should be able to tie down the phone at the last point of contact and then see where it pops up again along the route."

"Aren't those things illegal?" asked Alton.

"Only if you get caught, replied Ramirez, "And let's face it, this is for the greater good."

"Now, I still need those codes from you," asked Ramirez.

"Okay, but we must work together on this one," said Alton.

Ramirez had a plan.

He called NSA and they traced the phone signal from the driver of the second truck. To Alton's surprise, it had traversed Europe in the last couple of days and had made its way into the UK, via the Channel Tunnel.

Along the way, the truck had stopped near Ashford and from other phone signals, it looked as if there had been several extra people involved.

Ramirez looked at the additional identities which his NSA system had picked up. He had several additional numbers which he decided to share with Richard Alton.

"You are good," said Alton, "You've found a couple of SI6 phones in among all of the numbers."

He looked more carefully, realising his own phone was listed but then he noticed something odd. One of the phones listed was the contact number for Karen Martin.

Alton decided to keep this information to himself.

"That's incredible," thought Alton, "Just over two days by road from Israel to the UK. Intercepted and let go by us yet now the truck is parked somewhere around Birmingham."

Ed Adams

PART THREE

Event Management

To achieve great things, two things are needed:
a plan and not quite enough time.

-Leonard Bernstein

The gig

Bigsy drove the van to Christina's private party gig. They'd brought their musical equipment but the whole sound system had been prepared by the venue. It was one of the concert halls around Birmingham. The kind that was re-purposed for trade events.

It was a clever premise. The various key individuals had been invited but there was a kind of 'padding' of other people around the event, which had been billed as a kind of international trade congress, with evening entertainment.

Bigsy thought it was quite an elaborate method to get the various people into the country without raising particular suspicions. Sure enough, there were representatives from many nations, Europeans, Africans, Chinese and Americans. Bigsy had heard Russian being spoken and worked out quite quickly that many delegates were using English as a sort of international translation language.

The Square

Bigsy's team role was twofold. There was the main event to set up but also the small matter of ensuring that the various other rooms were also 'adjusted' for the meeting. This needed to be a fairly basic form of monitoring that would somehow get past the suspicions of anyone brought in to handle counter surveillance. Bigsy decided that it would be easiest to simply 'flaunt it' and hide his gadgets in plain sight. He did this by simply bringing small mixer desks with lots of lights into each room and securing them to the fixtures and fixings. They could be obviously 'on' with twinkling lights but also could easily and very obviously switched off. He had signs for them with 'do not switch off' which he suspected wouldn't buy him much but was worth a try.

'Do not switch off - dial 94 on the house phone for an engineer' - he hoped this would work.

Inside the devices he had arranged a small extra battery circuit. It would last around 9 hours once initiated and could digitally record sound without sending out radio signals. No radio signal meant it was virtually undetectable. It also meant it couldn't be used for live monitoring but did mean it could keep a record of whatever happened in the session.

He hoped this would work and that he would be able to gather suitable intelligence from the session.

The format of the day setup was fairly straightforward. There were a range of daytime sessions for 'the teams' from the various organisations present and then some evening entertainment. A few breakouts had been scheduled for the time between the day sessions and the evening's entertainment.

Bigsy was pretty sure that this would be the time when the discussion about the weapon would take place - that it would be on-site and in one of the break-out rooms. He had no-idea which one and had needed half a dozen of the mixer desks to cover the whole area.

He did notice that one other rooms seemed to be a little more well-appointed than the others and assumed that this would be the most likely one. He resisted the temptation to put additional equipment into it, on the basis that it also increased the chances of discovery.

The conference kicked off - with several well-known and quite controversial speakers. There were press present and they also seemed to have their own small room as part of the arrangements. There was also a special understanding about what could be put on the record and the participants seemed to be keeping the bargain around this.

Christina prepared for her gig. Bigsy noticed that Clare was going to be on stage as well, but he wasn't sure what she'd be doing there.

Then the bass kicked in and Christina was singing:

The Square

"I want to feel your body all over mine"
"I wanna get right to it, loving you…"

Bigsy blinked under the power output from the blaster lights but couldn't help but admire the way Christina had the audience in the palm of her hand.

Bigsy couldn't help but also notice that several of the representatives seemed to have particular teams of suited bodyguards around them. And that they seemed captivated by the music. He was not going to try to find out if they were effective, but they certainly looked like they enjoyed Christina's set.

The various breakout rooms were getting used. Most people just ignored the extra sound system available and were happy to sit around the table with its supply of coffee, fruit and pastries.

Bigsy made sure he was evident around the area as a part of the technical support for the event so that he did not suddenly appear at the time of the special assembly convening.

Sure enough, at around an hour before the close of the main day-time event, there was a meeting convened in the well-appointed room. Bigsy introduced himself and asked if they needed any special facilities.

"Actually, no, we have brought our own equipment for the next session. In fact, we would prefer that you switch off the projectors and other equipment."

Bigsy walked around powering everything down except the mixing desk. He would do this at a later stage. He left the room and could hear the people inside checking for electronics and microphones. They seemed amused that the room had so many obvious microphones present and were disconnecting them by hand.

Then Bigsy's phone rang.

"Hello, we would like you to return to the room, please." Bigsy agreed but deliberately waited around 10 minutes. He arrived holding his phone and looking busy.

"Please disable the mixer desk, we prefer no electronics except our own for the next session."

Bigsy nodded ostensibly still on the phone and moved towards the desk. He flipped a couple of switches and pressed a series of buttons in a very deliberate looking sequence, as if there needed to be a special disabling sequence. The desk lights went out and then Bigsy unplugged the cord from the back of it.

"There," he said, "Completely off. It's cabled into this position so I cannot physically remove it.".

The security people in the room looked at one another and thought that they now had a suitably disabled piece of equipment.

The Square

"That's fine," said one of them, "Now we'd appreciate it not to be disturbed for the next hour."

"OK - but you have my number if you need to call me," said Bigsy, pointing to the number displayed on the card.

Bigsy left and took up a position in an adjacent room. He left the door ajar enough to be able to see the comings and goings related to the other room. Sure enough, a short time later a group of people started to arrive. There were several groups in total and they seemed to comprise a mix of main players and some clearly heavy set support staff. Then the door closed and Bigsy could hear it locking.

Bigsy knew that his audio was working but would not dare to monitor it directly for fear of being caught. It was much better to check the recording later and away from the venue.

Now it was working, Bigsy had decided it was better to be further away and moved to a different room. He would have someone from the venue administration inform him when the meeting was finished.

Three hours later, his phone rang. It was the signal that the room was ready to be cleared. There would be no more meetings into the evening, when things would turn towards a mix of dining and entertainment. Bigsy suspected that the key people he had seen would be long gone by this time.

He collected the kit from the various rooms and moved it back to his van. It would be another hour before he could play it back, and that would be from another location completely. He manoeuvred the van through the dark streets of Birmingham and on his way to the meeting place outside of Birmingham.

Listening in

Bigsy had arrived at the hotel on the main toll road bypassing Birmingham.

There would be no reason to stay at this location except for people 'in transit' and the nearest facilities were the motorway services, a short walk from the hotel room.

Bigsy manoeuvred the small white van next to another one parked at the far corner of the car park. It was one he'd parked there earlier before picking up the one he'd driven into Birmingham. He swiftly moved the content of his current one to the new one and then re-parked the one he'd arrived in back in the main area of the car park. Both vans were on hire and he'd be paying a penalty to have the one that had gone into Birmingham picked up from the car park. The van switch was designed to reduce his chance of being followed based upon advice from Chuck.

Bigsy smiled as he thought back over the extra efforts to get new pay-as-you-go phones and the need for the van substitutions. Like a proper spy movie.

The whole exit from Birmingham had taken less than an hour and Bigsy now flipped the small memory card containing the recording into his hand. He'd go into his room in the hotel to listen to the playback, where Chuck and Clare would also join him.

Bigsy's small MacBook flicked into life and he plugged the card into its side and copied the recordings onto the computer. He swiftly copied them into another program and hit 'Play'.

Then he looked at the sound wave. There was a long period of relatively low activity, which sure, enough, was people arriving and settling down. He slid the recording forward to a more continuous series of activity and sure enough there was the start of a more formal meeting.

"One two."

"Gentlemen, thank you for taking the time to visit Birmingham today and I must apologise for the elaborate subterfuge. We wanted to ensure that all of the right parties had an opportunity to be part of this discussion and to be able to opt into what should be a highly profitable situation.

The Square

"You will all understand that we can't issue a prospectus for this, but we are looking for - 'Stakeholders' to be part of our plans. This is a little unconventional, and I'm sure that will appeal to the nature of many of your businesses.

"Put simply, we have acquired a weapon. Some would call it a 'Weapon of Mass Destruction'. I think we will call it a 'safeguard'.

"We intend to deploy it once to demonstrate that we are serious and to use it in a way that will provide gains to the interested parties within this room.

"The weapon contains a biohazard, one for which we have an antidote. It can remove populations quickly but once the antidote is applied, within a very short time a normal environment can be resumed.

"We intend to deploy this in a way that will be disruptive to a major city in a major economy. We intend to use it to drive economic chaos that can be advantageous to all of us that sign up to the programme.

"You have some decisions to make.

"Firstly, will you wish to be in on the process?

"Secondly, you have a vote about where we deploy the weapon based upon a nominated series of locations.

"Thirdly, we will be driving a particular currency to become stable and destroying two or three other ones based upon the outcome of this. You may nominate the preferred strong currency.

In case you wonder about any parts of this - we have arranged a small demonstration of the toxin. We also have an example of the antidote with us at this meeting. We will use another technique to create a diversion before we deploy the main toxin and we already have a countdown schedule arranged.

"You each have the option to join us and take a part in the decisions, then in the knowledge that you will be protected from the outcomes, both in terms of health and wealth.

"Or, you can choose to leave now, in which case you may know about this, you may even decide to tell others, but it will do you no good and, I can assure you, there will be suffering which will affect you directly as a consequence.

"It is regrettable if this sounds like a ransom request, it's better to think of it as an attractive offer for you and your various consortia, and that this is quite literally a 'once in a lifetime' situation.

"I shall give each of you thirty minutes now to consider. At the end of that time, anyone who does not wish to participate will be asked to leave. In this thirty minute period you will be asked to stay in the room. After those that decline have left, we will run our small 'product demonstration'.

"There was a clattering sound on the recording. Bigsy worked out it was the doors being secured in the room.

The crunch

Bigsy listened to the recording. It had quietened down and he could hear the mixed conversations of the groups in the room.

He fast forwarded the recording to when the volume raised again. It was around 30 minutes later.

"Hello, ladies, gentlemen," came the announcement.

"Let's see who wants to be in on this? I have arranged for the doors at the end of the room to be opened. If anyone needs to leave, now is the time."

Bigsy could hear some scraping of chairs and a few footsteps.

"There, it seems around ten people have decided that this opportunity is too rich for them, we can see each of them on the television screens. We set up a video link to that next room."

Next, you must each sample the BioPen. This is the antidote to the neurotoxin and a great form of defence.

Bigsy could hear the clink as what he imagined were the syringes of antidote being handed out.

"This is how you use the syringe, explained the voice. Hold it to your arm and press the small button. It should leave a small impression on your arm. A square of four dots where the needles fire.

"It is almost painless.

Bigsy heard a noise like a vacuum tube which repeated around a dozen times.

"That's great, you are now all inoculated from the nerve agent."

"Let's see what it does. Watch the television monitors."

There was a silence and then a muffled scream. Bigsy worked out it was coming from the TV monitor relayed from the next room.

He listened for several minutes and was aware that the people in the room with the recording had gone quiet.

"There, you can see just how effective this agent is. No-one survived. Now we will open the doors to this room," There were cries of "No, Stop!"

"You are all forgetting that you are immune to the agent. The injection has rendered the nerve agent useless against each of you."

Bigsy could hear the doors being unbolted. There was movement as if of feet running.

"See," said the voice, "You are all unharmed.
Furthermore, in a half hour the neurotoxin will have been rendered harmless. Until that time, no-one unprotected should go into either of these rooms. That is why we are keeping the outer perimeter doors locked."

"Now we need to talk about the price of continued admission to this very select club."

Bigsy realised what had happened. The nerve agent had been demonstrated, the antidote had been shown to work and now the representatives were being asked for money.

"I think we will set the admission price in US dollars. Let us say 10 million."

Bigsy could hear the hubbub as people discussed this and he realised they had all worked out that there would be a higher price to pay if they didn't accept. This was no auction. It was simply holding the players to ransom.

"Think you should appoint a spokesperson and then let us know your response within the hour. It is 15:30 now, we will return at 16:30. Some of you will pay and others may wish to visit another of our rooms."

Bigsy called through to Chuck.

"Chuck, I have the recording; it was not an auction. It was a ransom. Pay $10 million for a piece of the action or become a lab experiment for the toxin. They just killed the people who opted out and have threatened the rest. My guess is that they will make around $100 million from this one deal."

Chuck replied, "Do we know if the rest of the toxin is here? Or was it just enough for the demonstration?"

"I don't know, they asked where people would like it to be used - for example in a major city - and which currency they would like to affect. This takes terrorism to a whole new level."

Chuck relayed the information on to Jake and Clare and then called Richard Alton.

"Richard, they have the toxin here in Birmingham. We are also concerned that they have another supply of it somewhere else and are getting ready to deploy it."

"Okay, my source, a Major Ramirez, in Washington, tells me that the threat is planned for London. He has been asked by Colonel Carson to come over to London to co-ordinate American involvement. Carson is heading for Frankfurt, where there is another large US control station."

"Ramirez says he thinks the second truck came across mainland Europe, through a significant number of major cities. Look, I've some other news. James wants to come back to support you in the next stage."

"James? I'd have thought he was well out of it now?"

"No, we've agreed to keep Léa safe, but James says he considers the mission as unfinished business. He's asked to meet up with you again in Birmingham."

"Sure," said Chuck, "He knows his own mind. Send him along. We're at the Hyatt Regency Birmingham. We'll see him tomorrow."

Under Pressure

*He who cannot stand the heat
should stay out of the kitchen.*

Harry S. Trueman

Ramirez thoughts

Ramirez was still thinking about Truck 2. It had traversed Europe. It could have delivered some of the containers to an intermediate city on its way through.

He placed a call to Alford.

"Hi Robert,"

"Hi Ramirez, the truck has finally arrived in Birmingham. At least that is what my people are saying. I've also got a recording from one of Chuck Manner's friends."

"I'm slightly surprised that your own NSA hasn't picked up on this. Why didn't Carson know this? He'd have expected to have received the intel from the NSA faster than from the Brits."

It made Ramirez wonder whether there was any form of delay being introduced.

Ramirez also considered the BioPens. It seemed that the BioPens had found their way to the Birmingham venue, at least according to the information that he had received from Alton.

Once again, nothing from Carson. Ramirez began to wonder whether there was some kind of mute switch being applied to the information about these consignments.

He took a closer look at the delay around Ashford, on the way between Dover and London. There had been intense activity around this point, although the toxin transfer had continued.

It looked as if some of the people at this rendezvous had moved back towards London, but that others had continued on the way to Birmingham.

The challenge was, which items had gone to which location?

Fortunately, now that Alton had phoned, Ramirez could do some hunting. He knew that both the toxin and at least several of the BioPens were in Birmingham.

"Look Robert, I'm going to need to be able to talk directly to your contact in Birmingham. That's Colonel Chuck Connors, isn't it?"

"Yes, I'll send you his phone details. I'll also let him now that he should expect a call from you."

Unexpected guest

Chuck was in the bar at the hotel when James arrived.

"You must be crazy!" greeted Chuck.

"I sometimes wonder," said James.

"You've met Jake, I'll have to introduce you to the creators of sound effects during Léa's rescue," said Chuck.

He gestured across to another table. Bigsy, Jake and Clare turned and waved.

"I thought I'd introduce you in stages!" said Chuck, as the others walked across.

"Hey again," said Jake, "I guess they found somewhere to squirrel you away, in London?"

"I'm under great pains to not disclose locations," said James, "You know how it is."

"Not really," said Bigsy, "Hi I'm Bigsy and helped manufacture that soundscape for the extraction!" I used some CSI banter and a couple of comedy cop movies to create the frantic mission effect."

"Well it did the trick," said James, "And you must be Clare!"

Clare grinned, "Yes and I'm pleased you all got through that tricky extraction. I'd expect no less if you get mixed up with Chuck Manners though."

James replied, "I'm not surprised you are in this rather spiffy hotel, either. It is typical of a well-off freelancer or a high-end government official."

"And in case you are wondering, I think I owe it to all of you to try to see this thing through now," said James.

"It's interesting for a freelancer to think like that," said Chuck.

"Yes, but if you think about it, I'll still want more work from the UK government, so it's better that I get a gold star, rather than a question mark in my report."

The bar was filling. A trade convention of salesmen had arrived and were busy slapping one another on the back. Adjacent to the bar, James could see a dining area. It looked positively peaceful.

Then he noticed something.

"My god!" he whispered, "Don't look now, but that's Karen," he gestured to a woman sitting alone in the restaurant.

"But Karen was murdered with a sniper rifle?" asked Chuck.

"I'm telling you, that is Karen. I need to get away from here, she doesn't know any of you."

James moved across the bar, past the salesmen and towards the exit from the area. Chuck could see he was by the elevators, and then gone.

"We need to check this out," said Clare, "I'll go in and check," she walked away pressing buttons on her phone. They could see Clare reading the menu outside of the restaurant area. Then they saw her take a photograph of the menu, turn around and walk across to the bar.

"She's trying to separate herself from us," said Chuck, "Let's go to that other lounge area over there, the one without the bar."

Jake and Bigsy stood and the three of them strolled nonchalantly towards a seating area away from the bar. Clare moved across to re-join them.

"I've got her photo, here," she said, "I'll share it with you all."

Chuck reached for his phone and took an AirDrop copy of the photograph.

"I'm going to send this on to Robert Alton for positive confirmation," he said.

He sent a short message to Alton and they all waited, slightly unsure of their next move.

A text came back to Chuck's phone.

"Confirmed, it is Karen Martin."

"Very interesting," said Chuck, "It can only mean that Karen is involved in the biggest plan."

"This has to be money motivated," said Jake. "Or else why would she do it. Ideological reasons? I don't think so. Pressure applied? Maybe."

"The sort of money they were talking about for the pre-funding was huge, in any case," said Bigsy, "Several partners-in-crime, each putting up $10 million. I guess Karen might only get small slice, but it is still a lot of cash."

"Okay," said Chuck, "We have a couple of options. To observe her or to reel her in?"

"Well she is very close at the moment, I presume she could easily hide from us if she realised we were on to her."

"I agree," said Chuck. I think we must corral her and find out what is happening. I'm going to contact Robert Alton again and clear this with him."

He picked up his phone and walked away into a corner of the room.

Bigsy and Clare thought of a plan.

"I'll go to the restaurant. I can get an adjacent table," said Clare.

"I can get a table by the exit," said Bigsy.

"And Chuck can cover us from the back. We can't use James for this, because she will recognise him."

Chuck returned. "I've spoken to Robert Alton. He is quite relaxed about us pulling Karen but would like an opportunity to talk to her himself."

"We are going into the restaurant, once we have her, we can take her to your room in the hotel."

"I'll engage her in conversation first," said Clare, "We need to stop her from running away."

"I'm going to explain this to the restaurant staff," said Chuck, "It's time to flash a badge."

He walked towards the restaurant to seek the manager.

Then Clare wandered towards a table and asked to be seated at one very close to Karen. Bigsy followed and then Chuck took a seat much further away at the other end of the restaurant.

Karen briefly looked up, but then continued to read her phone. She was waiting for a next course to arrive.

"Excuse me," said Clare, "I hope you don't mind me asking this, but I've been chatted up by several of the men in the sales conference. Could you keep an eye out for me in case anyone tries to follow me in here?"

Karen smiled, "Yes, I'll keep a lookout, but I think the staff here are very good and they will ensure that you are not the source of unwanted attention."

Clare smiled, "That's the thing. We think you might also be the source of something. Is your name Karen?"

Karen tensed, "No, I think you have made a mistake?"

Bigsy moved from his table and Chuck stood. Karen looked around. She could assess the odds at three declared to her one.

The Square

"Look, what is the about?" she asked.

"I think you had better come with us," said Chuck, "I think we know something you will want to hear."

Karen looked around; she realised that escape would be difficult. The staff in the restaurant appeared to be taking the scene in their stride and she realised that they had been badged or briefed in some way.

"Okay, I'll come along," she said, "I don't know who you are or what you want, but you have the wrong person."

They all moved towards the elevators. Chuck used his special access key to the executive floors. Clare and Bigsy looked at one another, they just knew that Chuck would have a suite.

In a few moments they were entering the room. Karen remained very calm and unruffled by this strange behaviour. Chuck was on the phone to James and a few moments later he arrived at the door of Chuck's room.

"Hello Karen," said James, "I was expecting to see you in Cairo."

Karen looked towards James; they could all see that her last opportunity to bluff through this situation had just evaporated.

"James," she said, "This is most unexpected."

"You will need to tell us, to tell us all, what is happening and what is your part?"

Unbelievable

Karen began, "Okay, you know I've been a loyal member of SI6 for many years. I've been put under pressure in the middle east on numerous occasions. I was working with a guy called Fredericksson in Istanbul. He was supposedly from American intelligence but didn't have the moves that I'd expect. I thought all along that he had been wildcatted into the mission.

"We were to extract a small cell of American undercover agents. They were Muslim and had been able to work across the borders into Iraq and Iran, mainly intelligence gathering. Something had gone wrong and they had been discovered. One of them was killed in Iraq. A most bloody turn of events conducted under the ISIL penal code.

"A beheading?" asked James.

"That's right," said Karen, "A televised beheading. To keep everyone else in their place."

Clare shuddered, "How awful."

"Yes, I felt responsible for the whole cell. It had been my job to place them in Iraq and now it was my duty to get them freed again."

"It's brutal in some of these countries," said Chuck, "I've seen the hangings and beheadings in Riyadh too. They even push westerners to the front in so-called Chop-Chop Square, to show them what happens if we misbehave; it runs at something like 150 executions per year. That's three a week. It's where the phrase 'blood money' comes from. In a murder, the family of the murderer can pay the victim family blood money to atone for the crime. "

"Yes," said James, "and the Testament that those to be executed utter, it brings us back neatly to Karen."

"No, I'm not going along the Shahadah route," said Karen, "Or before I know it my head will be rolling several metres from my body."

Clare grimaced at this, "Can we get back to Karen's explanation?"

"Well, I was threatened, by, of all people, my own bosses - or, I should say, one boss in particular - Carson."

"He told me that I should take personal responsibility for the exfiltration of the agents. That they needed to be brought back intact and that they were valuable assets. To my eyes, they were burned assets. We could never send them back into such a scenario again."

"I arranged for an extraction, from Istanbul. It was supposed to be very low key. I took the team of them through the commercial airport on regular passenger tickets. We all arrived at İstanbul Havalimanı - which is the main airport and were checked in to a flight to Washington. Nothing suspicious, regular amounts of luggage and no tools of the trade.

"Tools of the trade?" asked Clare.

"Weapons or suspicious items in our baggage," replied Karen, "Three of the guys were greeted at the airport by hospitality people. They said they had been upgraded and would be able to fly in the front of the plane. First Class. I was wary of this, but let it go ahead. The others were escorted to the business lounge at the airport. They were told that they had not made the upgrade but that the lounge was the least they could do. That was another four, plus me, left to go in economy."

"It has all the hallmarks of a trap," stated James. Chuck nodded agreement.

Karen continued, "Of course, the other four were delighted to spend some time in the lounge and followed the hospitality people. That left just me - the woman. It was over an hour to the flight, so I went to sit in the cafe area downstairs in the terminal.

"Then I noticed a black military truck outside the glass windows. All seven of the men were being loaded onto it.

Karen continued, "A man approached me. I was adrenalined out at this point and worried that this could be my grim reaper. He was softly spoken. Said his name was Fredericksson. Told me that the seven would disappear, but that I was to be left to go about my business. That the story of their disappearance would be of a lurid rounding up, well before I got to the airport. In effect the men had not disappeared in my care.

"In return he said he didn't want anything at this time, but that he would be back at some point for a favour. He didn't say what it was, or who he worked for."

Chuck and James looked at one another. It was clear that they couldn't work out where Fredericksson had come from.

Karen continued, "Years have gone past since that event, but I still think of it every day. How seven men in my care were loaded onto a truck and taken away to be executed.

"Then, around a couple of months ago, I was contacted by Fredericksson again. He said he remembered me and the touching scene at the airport. He now had something he wanted me to do. He explained that a Colonel Carson would be in contact. It was about a truck carrying - he said - missiles from Israel across Egypt. I was to do what I was asked by Carson and should expect to disappear at the end of the mission. He put it that if I did it well, then I would survive and simply disappear. If I did it badly, then it would be curtains.

"That's when I was asked to exchange the briefcase in the desert, via a stringer- you James. I didn't think it could be that complex, so I agreed.

"Did they offer to pay you anything for any of this?" asked Chuck.

"No, the only payment was their silence, my guilt and my life, including anonymity," answered Karen.

"I think Ramirez works for someone called Carson," said Chuck, "we had better be very careful with this information."

"Couldn't you have told someone, somewhere?" asked Clare looking at Karen.

"I suppose I could have right at the beginning, but I was so scared then, having seen several good people put onto a truck. - It would have destroyed my service career too, I suppose that doesn't seem important to most of you, but it is a very complicated life that we all lead in this line of work."

Clare shuddered again.

Jake looked at Bigsy, "Don't you feel any remorse?" asked Jake, "For those men or what you have got into now?"

"It completely ran away from me," said Karen. "Just think about it, I'm asked to pass a case to a lorry driver via a stringer - no big deal. The next thing I know I'm caught up in some death threat to wipe out half of London."

"So, do you know the plans of Al Aktar?" asked Jake.

"Spell it?" asked Karen.

"A-L space A-K-T-A-R," responded Jake.

"Al Aktar - That's surely a bit of badge engineering?" said Karen, "You know in Arabic it means "the most", but its only a letter away from a Pakistani outfit called Al Akhtar, which have been mujahideen supporters, providing quarter-mastering under the guise of humanitarian aid."

"No, I don't know their plans, but I suspect they have been produced as scapegoats for whatever threat has been laid down."

"So, what do you know then?" asked Chuck. "You must have been told something, to make you come back here?"

The Square

"They told me that there were two consignments to be dispatched to London. A cylinder, which contains a toxin and a set of smaller units which are antidotes - mini-syringes if you will. They told me that the codes to activate were originally in the case which James was to hand over to the truck driver."

"So, we have a perfect storm?" asked Jake," The cylinders, carrying toxins, the arm codes and the antidotes all bound for London?"

"That's right," said Karen, "and I've seen each of the item be dispatched during today."

"What have we got?" asked Chuck, "Number plates, types of vehicle, endpoints?"

"Nothing," said Karen, "I've got nothing. I could see the dispatch from here in the hotel. On a tv monitor wired into my room in the hotel. I couldn't even swear that the dispatch was from Birmingham."

"At least we have got London, " said Chuck.

"And we know that the antidotes are individually RFID'd" said Bigsy, "That should make them easier to track down."

Carson and Ramirez

Chuck's phone rang. It was Robert Alton.

"Hey Chuck, I wanted to let you know the latest. I've a contact in the Pentagon, a Colonel Ramirez. He has been following your situation and trying to trace the trucks. I have told him about you, and he is likely to call you sometime soon."

Chuck commented, "We need to find out whose side he is on. He receives direct orders from Carson but may not be aware of Carson's role in all of this."

"Meaning what?" asked Alton.

Chuck continued, "We've been with Karen."

"Karen?" Alton sounded surprised, "Karen's phone turned up at one of the truck rendezvous points. It made me wonder if she was still around. How is she?"

"She seems fine - the shooter was working for her and the hit was staged. She has told us about the situation as well as how she became implicated. Part of it has been to tell us that Colonel Carson is not what he seems. Karen has him pegged as an opportunist, working for a guy called Fredericksson."

"It also casts a shadow over Ramirez. He appears to work directly for Carson."

Alton continued, "Many people have been wary of Carson for a long time. He acts with political will and keeps much of what he is doing secret. A lot of people in Washington don't trust him, although I don't think they'd expect him to be working for another state actor.

"I don't think Ramirez is aware of the depth on this situation, Carson was talking about sending Ramirez to London, to supervise the operation more closely. I doubt whether Ramirez would go if he knew what was planned for London? Additionally, Ramirez has told me that Carson is planning to go to Frankfurt. Strangely co-incidental?

Alton added, "Something else, I was out on a mission yesterday. We caught some local lads moving BioPens around. We detained them just outside of Ashford. They were handing the devices over to a group of Arabs."

Chuck said, "This is very useful. I think we can assume that London is being targeted, and that perhaps Frankfurt will be the centre for financial trading during the disruption. Look - we'll be in London soon. It would be best to meet with you there. How about Westminster?"

"Certainly," replied Alton, "You couldn't get much closer!"

Ed Adams

Triangulation stations

"The only people who can see the whole picture," he murmured, "are the ones who step out of the frame."

— Salman Rushdie

Showdown mechanics

Karen asked, "What about those BioPens you mentioned. What are they?"

"Don't you know?" asked James. Karen shook her head.

"They are antidotes to the cylinders of nerve agent. They were smuggled in ahead of the main cylinders of nerve agent that were on the two trucks"

Karen looked confused, "What two trucks? Not the one I sent James to intercept? I was told this truck carried a missile."

"Yes, but that was yet another layer of deception, the truck was carrying the nerve agent. James had the unlock codes for the nerve agent, which was a binary."

"And the BioPens?"

"They provide the antidote to the nerve agent."

Chuck could see that the situation was registering with Karen. She realised she had been told something different and was having to re-piece the story together now.

"Wagons roll," Chuck declared, "We are all going to London, right now."

.-- ....--. -....- -.-. .-. .- -.-. -.- / .- .-- .- -.—

Two and a half hours later they were in Central London and driving into a car park underneath College Green, adjacent to the Houses of Parliament.

"We could hardly be more central," said Chuck. Jake nodded agreement.

He had driven the silver BMW hire car and Bigsy drove the black one. Now they were conveniently parked and ready to meet Alton.

Karen was in Bigsy's car, with James who had told her in no uncertain terms not to attempt to escape.

Chuck was already on the phone to Alton, "We're here, in Westminster - can we meet along Millbank?"

"Sure thing, How about Ravello's coffee bar - it's on Horseferry Road, just up from MI5."

Chuck said out loud, "Ravello's."

"I know it," said Jake, "Up from Lambeth Bridge. Less than ten minutes by foot."

"We'll see you there, in around ten minutes," said Chuck.

They walked to the small coffee bar, past the entrance to MI5, which Jake pointed out for everyone else. As they entered, Bigsy spotted a large group of tables and pulled two together.

Clare went to the counter to order some drinks. As she returned to sit down, the whole group were sat around the two tables, with a couple of spaces, which she assumed were for her and for Alton.

"We are suddenly quite a large group," she said.

At that moment Chuck stood, "Robert," he called.

Robert Alton smiled and looked over. He saw Karen in the group and his face hardened.

"Hello Chuck," he said, "Hello Karen, we all thought you were dead - not involved in some terrorist plot."

"Chuck, I brought a couple of friends who are waiting outside," Alton looked pointedly towards Karen.

"So what do we know?" he asked, "A terrorist plot to unleash US nerve gas modifications in central London.

Financial manipulations. Carson involved. The binary to be mobilised with the codes from the briefcase. But we don't know where."

"That's about the shape of it," said Chuck.

"One thing," said Bigsy, "We know the BioPens were tracker enabled, with active RFID encoding."

"That's not enough to mean that GCHQ or anyone could track them down, but with a blast of radar at the right frequency, we should be able to spot a whole cluster of the pens."

"How would we achieve that?" asked Alton, "It sounds like mad science."

Bigsy grinned, "not really, your Typhoons have advanced radar on them, usually used for targeting. It's called Paveway, I think. If several Typhoons flew over London and used their targeting systems, we could possibly triangulate the RFIDs from the BioPens.

"Hmm, I'm not sure of this as a plan," said Alton, "nor am I certain that I could whistle up several Typhoon fighters."

"They have flown jet fighters along the Thames in the past," said Clare, "For big celebrations, like Royal Anniversaries."

"Wait," said Jake, "There's a meeting in London today. Some kind of government financial forum - the World

Financial Forum - Could the planes be a useful added feature?"

"That might also be a clue," said Clare, "Disrupt finance whilst the WFF are meeting in London?"

"Okay," said Alton, "This could be my career defining moment. I'm patching through to Operations Centre, to see where we can rustle up some planes. Bigsy, I'll need you on the call to help explain all of this to the centre."

Bigsy nodded, "It's simple really, instead of the planes having their targets 'lit' by a beam, they will be looking for the beam generated by the RFIDs on each of the BioPen vials.. Those antibodies used active tags. That means they will be in the 433 MHz frequency range. I just hope that the Typhoon sensors can go that low. We are almost into shopping cart territory."

Alton could see that Bigsy was rapidly scrolling through what appeared to be a car brochure, but was actually a brochure for the $35m Eurofighter Typhoon.

"We ideally need two sweeps, he added, One along the river and another north London to south. That way we can triangulate the findings."

Alton grimaced,"It's not going to be that simple. I've been told we can have three planes and that they can pass once along the Thames. North to south isn't possible though, it cuts right across the Heathrow flight path."

"Go with it," said Chuck, "we'll see where we are after the first pass."

Alton said, "No wait, the RAF have come back with a counter offer. It's a Sentinel R1, which is already airborne and could be over London in about ten minutes. It can fly high and across London."

"The Sentinel?" asked Chuck, "They were used in Afghanistan against pop-up targets. I didn't know there were still any out there."

Bigsy was scrolling through more pages on the internet. "I see," he said, "They have a sensor bulge to track for targets. The radar it uses is quite an old system, but I suppose the active RFID is also quite old technology."

"Right," said Alton, "We'll have one pass over with the Sentinel north to south and then the scrambled Typhoons flying up the Thames. It's our best shot at this. It'll all be over in about 20 minutes."

They scrutinised a map of London and the intended course of the two sets of planes. Trying to guess where the sensors might be located.

Alton's phone rang.

"It's the feedback from the Sentinel. It has flown over London and says it seems to be acquiring active RFIDs from 51.51,-0.08 That's over the City of London."

They scrutinised the map. Bigsy typed the co-ordinates into his laptop.

"It seems to be St Mary Axe," he said, "that's the Gherkin tower."

"It is also where the WFF Conference is taking place," added Jake.

"How accurate are these sweeps?" asked Chuck.

"Without triangulation, they claim to be only to within a couple of street blocks," answered Alton.

"Listen," said Clare, "She ran to the door of the cafe and looked along the street.

"That was the Typhoons! I saw them fly past the end of the road. They were low!"

As she spoke, Alton's phone rang again.

"We just got the Typhoons' readings, 51.513929, -0.0883573. They say it is a sample of the three. It comes out at the Bank of England.

Jake looked at the map, "Yes, that makes sense. The latitude of the Gherkin and the Bank of England are almost identical."

Chuck stared at the map. "So, this road - Threadneedle Street - runs between the two areas? I'm going to take a look."

To everyone's surprise, Chuck walked out of the cafe and hailed a London black cab.

"Well, I suppose it is the fastest way to get there," said Jake.

"And pollution free, now they are electric," added Clare.

Right, now I think, Karen, it is time for you to say goodbye to these people and to come with my colleagues. You'll recognise the building we are taking you to."

Karen nodded. She knew she had run out of road.

Alton stayed behind.

Bank

Chuck arrived at the busy road junction in London known as Bank. The taxi driver dropped him off on the triangle of land adjacent to the Duke of Wellington statue. Ahead were the steps leading up to The Royal Exchange.

"The Bank of England is across the road there," said the cabby, pointing towards the front entrance.

Chuck paid with his card and climbed out. There was an amount of disruption on the pavement. He could see that a new art installation was being installed on the concourse of the Royal Exchange.

He looked again, there were several bearded workmen around in high visibility jackets. He noticed they were of middle eastern origin. He could see the cylindrical artwork and realised that it was the missing canister, which had been hastily sprayed with a dull metallic finish.

The Square

Chuck called Alton,"It's here, the canister. I think the antidotes will be in the truck that is parked in the sidewalk outside the Royal Exchange."

Chuck looked towards the Bank of England. The canister was placed to be directly outside. If it was allowed to release the nerve agent, there would be a huge disaster in this part of the City.

There was a news feed on an adjacent building. It was scrolling that an airstrike had been attempted on Heathrow. Chuck thought that it signified the start of the terrorist distraction plan.

Ravello's cafe had BBC News channel scrolling across it. The latest updates were about the attempted attack on Heathrow. But that three RAF fighter planes had intercepted the missiles and then located the original attackers. No-one explained why the three Typhoon planes were flying across that part of London at the right time.

.--- ..- -- .--. / -.-. ..- - / - --- / ..-. .-. .- -. -.- ..-. ..- .-. —

In Frankfurt, Carson was sitting in the control room, waiting to start running the trader scripts. He could see that the plan was unravelling. The diversion had been intercepted. He didn't know whether the nerve gas would work. He decided he would need to take over control of the London site.

The London truck had been wired for a conventional bomb as well as the nerve gas. Carson had a phone number to trigger the bomb. He dialled it.

Chuck heard a phone ringing in the truck and ran towards the Tube's subway entrance. There was an almighty explosion and the truck was lifted several feet into the air. The men who had been installing the artwork didn't live to tell the tale.

The cylinder had been fractured and now a green fluid was leaking onto the ground from where it soon evaporated. Emergency sirens moved towards the area and a rapid response team dressed in Hazardous Material suits from the City of London started to cordon the area.

... --- ...

Clare, Bigsy, James and Alton could see events unfolding from the television in Ravello's. As TV crews arrived, they noticed the fractured cylinder and wondered why it had not created more havoc.

Alton was on the phone. "Yes, good, clear. Thank you."

He turned to the group.

"We had to keep it quiet, but we'd swapped the codes to the cylinders when Chuck brought in the case from James."

"We swapped the 'arm' codes for 'disarm' codes. They still looked right and registered on the device, but they had the effect to neutralise rather than excite the cylinders."

"Do you mean Chuck raced all across London for nothing?"

"Not quite. Chuck knew about the exchange of the codes. He also knew how much we wanted to get these terrorists brought in."

Alton continued, "I have just had it confirmed that we have also found Carson in Frankfurt. He was sitting in a financial trading desk waiting for the shares and financial position to go crazy. We can link him directly to the phone call which exploded the truck bomb."

"What about Fredericksson?" asked Clare.

"No, we still don't know who he is, or who he works for. Maybe when we have Carson, we can find out some more. Don't forget we also have Karen Martin now."

"And Chuck? How is Chuck after the explosions around Bank?" asked Jake.

Alton looked stony faced, "Chuck would prefer to be gone," he replied, "Later on today we will find Chuck's green suit as the remnants from the explosion."

"Okay, I hear you," said Bigsy, "Chuck has disappeared on us again."

"I think he would like it to be thought that he had been blown up by the truck bomb," said Alton.

James looked at Clare, who looked quite tearful.

"I get the impression that you all liked Chuck?"

"A lot," answered Clare.

Jake and Bigsy nodded.

The Anchor

Jake, Clare and Bigsy were sitting around a raised table in the Anchor pub. It looked out onto the River Thames, close to the city and central London.

"Tom Cruise made a movie that included this pub," said Bigsy.

"Well, it is kind of scenic," said Clare, "with that view of St Paul's Cathedral."

"I doubt whether his impossible mission was as complex as ours," said Jake.

"But I'll bet our mission is just as secret as anything that MI5 would run," added Bigsy.

"And we'll still be waiting to hear from out mysterious disappearing Colonel Manners again," said Jake.

"Or that Robert Alton, maybe, or even James." Said Bigsy, "Hey, look, here comes Christina, we'll have to tell her all about this one."

"She'll never believe us," said Clare.

Lightning Source UK Ltd.
Milton Keynes UK
UKHW020025310520
364100UK00005B/924